The Scoundrel and the Satyr King

A MM MONSTER REGENCY ROMANCE

A MONSTERS BALL NOVELLA

CLIO EVANS

There are monster balls and Monster Balls, and this story has both.

Author's Note

This author must report that the following have been discovered in the Scoundrel and the Satyr King:

Monstrous cocks, hate sex, breeding kinks, assault (not by either main character), insta-love, bondage, wax play, dueling with guns, and more.

I would also like to note that while this story takes place in the regency era, there have been some changes made to the "rules" of society, such as allowing gay marriage. This is a fictionalized version of the regency time period (and a lot more fun than real history).

- Their Majesty Clio Evans

The Queen's Invitation

Land of Essex, 1823

Pan

"Your Majesty, a letter has arrived from Her Majesty Queen Charlotte of England."

"Oh, excellent," I chuckled, excitement bursting through me.

I'd been expecting a letter from Lottie for some time now, wondering when the plan would come to fruition.

I grinned at Bernard, my most loyal and honest servant. He was not a Satyr like me but a very stout Minotaur who was surprisingly agile. He handed the envelope to me, not even blinking at the fact that I was lounging undressed in the spring that was in my outdoor garden. No, it was not uncommon to find the Satyr King naked in his own home. The only time I actually made an effort to wear clothing was when a human visited— especially those from London's esteemed society. The lords and ladies of England did not share the same indulgent views as the creatures of the Lands of Essex.

One of my favorite memories as of late was when one of the Queen's letter boys had made a visit in the middle of an orgy at the castle, one that had lasted three days. The poor lad had left trembling in his trousers and tongue tied by one of the nymphs who had taken a liking to him.

I was known far and wide as a king that enjoyed sex, debauchery, and, on occasion, the mundane pleasures of this world. Even after centuries of being a King, I had never lost my zeal for life. I was a scandal, but the kind that the ton lived for. And who would challenge a King for his wild tastes when he was the most charming and beloved in all of his lands? Unlike the rakes that were frowned upon in society, I was looked upon as a god of delight.

All of that would soon change, though, if I could not find a suitable partner.

Turning my attention back to the letter that had been delivered, I broke the wax seal and read the elegantly scrawled lines, seeing that our recent conversation had come to fruition. In my hands was the invitation to the Monster's Ball—an event for the nobility of monsters and humans alike. One of four that would be taking place, with me attending the June offering.

"This will be most excellent," I said. "I will find a suitable mate here, and my brother can cease his pointless threats."

My brother, the only one in this world that liked to shite on my sunshine.

2

"He will not triumph, Your Majesty," Bernard said. "You are most beloved by everyone. A god to the mortals, and a worshipped member of High Society. You are a caring and good—"

"My dear friend," I laughed, cutting him off. "I simply cannot hear anymore of your wagging tongue. I appreciate you dearly, but let us allow others to give me such words. Is your daughter joining the ton of London next season?"

"She is, Sir" he said, his expression that of a proud father. "She has been talking my ear off every chance she gets, asking for the latest on London dit."

"She will do wonderfully," I said. "Being a Monster is quite fashionable now, I hear. Even if your King is a royal roué."

Bernard feigned a gasp, before it was followed by a chuckle.

I smiled, leaning back in the water and looking up at the beautiful sky. "Fetch my robe, Bernard, we have much to prepare. Oh, and acquire me the guest attendance list. I must see what the market holds for me."

Dishonour to the Duke

London, June 1823

E zra

MY HEAD WAS POUNDING SOMETHING FIERCE, MY BODY jostling back and forth. The scent of cologne and tobacco surrounded me, slowly rousing me from my slumber.

The thought suddenly struck me that I should have been in my chambers, not in...wherever here was.

My eyes flew open with a growl, and I sat straight up, alert and ready to fight whomever this dandy was.

"John Ezra Fitzroy III."

The sneer alone sent my heart thrashing, and even though I felt like I had just crawled out of one of London's pubs, I steeled my emotions and faced the man that I loathed.

"Father," I hissed.

Sitting across from me, I could not help but notice our similarities, both tall and well-built, with caramel brown hair. But where I had gotten into the habit of veiling my emotions, Duke John Ezra Fitzroy II was perpetually filled with furious indignation, more often than not at my expense.

Right at this moment, his piercing blue gaze was unwavering, the anger palpable.

The air around us shimmered with it, the tension between a father and son who had never seen eye to eye on anything.

I had done many things in my time of being a grown man, and most of them had been forgivable.

Being part of London's elite certainly had its perks—and being the scandal the ton liked to discuss with their afternoon tea made it worth the dirty looks I received.

I didn't choose this life for myself and sometimes imagined that one day my father would disown me and bestow his righteous expectations on his other progeny with his fresh duchess.

Instead, I remained the sole heir of his rage, which meant that he liked to retrieve me from my liaisons himself.

I knew my wishes were for naught however, nothing more than youthful desires despoiled by noblesse oblige. I was supposed to embrace my birthright and take pride in my family's illustrious history with the Crown, but the truth was it all made me incredibly tired just thinking about the burden that would soon be mine to shoulder.

I had earned the reputation of being a rake, and while the label came with its allowances, I also did not wish for my ill repute to harm others, so I was resigned about the prospect of dukedom.

My head continued to ache as I attempted to recall where I had last been.

In fact, the very last thing I remembered was escaping the Gentleman's Club where I had been playing a game of commerce with my wild cousin, Phoebe. Just as her father, my uncle James, had burst in, I had slipped out and was met with my father's butler...more specifically the butt of his pistol as it rammed me in the back of the skull. The two Dukes had jumped us themselves, and were undoubtedly now the ton's fresh gossip of the sennight.

Shite, I had left the lady all alone too.

I felt a tremor of guilt for a moment but then remembered Phoebe Fitzroy was no damsel in distress, and was perfectly able to handle her own father. My cousin had already taken her place in society, definitely not as London's elite might have expected of a *lady*, rather she was called "wild" and "the bane of English womanhood". I regretted that for her as she had more gumption than half the bastards this side of London and certainly more class than the audience of gossips.

The Fitzroys had a reputation beholden to our fathers— Duke John and Lord James Fitzroy, sons of Duke Ezra Fitzroy I. While the Fitzroy family had an illustrious history, the two brothers had upheld the generational reputation, joining the upper echelons of London society and becoming advisors to Her Majesty herself.

Our family businesses were spread throughout London; exotic cigars, well-renowned tailors, and, of course our notable, 'Fitzroy Gin'. We owned land outside of the main city and in other parts of Britain as well, but our family had called London home as far back as I could remember.

I was the eldest son to Duke John Fitzroy II, which meant I had been served on a golden platter for both my father and London society to scrutinize. I had spent my entire life trying to live up to my father's expectations until the passing of my mother.

From then on, it had seemed ridiculous and pointless to be a pillar of righteous nobility, and instead I had partaken in all the rabble-rousing I could find myself in—a true hellion by societal standards if I ever saw one.

"You have gone too far, Sir," I snarled, leaning for the door to the carriage.

The end of my father's cane cracked against the back of my hand and I swiftly pulled it back with a hiss, the pain stinging.

"No, boy, *you* have gone too far," he growled. "You have one purpose. One. To attend the Monster's Ball as Her Majesty has asked tomorrow eve and to not destroy your reputation any further."

"That's two reasons, Sir."

The noise that my father made was almost inhuman. "You are to restore the dishonour you have brought—"

"*Me*?" I sputtered, scoffing.

"Yes, *you*!" he thundered, his face turning beet red.

He leaned forward in his seat to sneer every word.

"You are the eldest son of a Duke! A Duke that is beloved by Her Majesty the Queen. Our family has rightfully earned its respect and standing in society, and you will not destroy what I–and my father and his father before that–have so ardently established. You are to inherit my title, but not if you continue on this wretched path of self-destruction; I will not let the whims of a boy dismantle the Fitzroy family. Everything you touch turns to ruin, including your mother. Do you truly wish to join the filth of the slums?"

The mention of my mother made my chest ache, but I did not dare tear my gaze away from my father. The only way to know where a lion would strike was by looking it in the eye, and turning my attention from him at this moment would only allow him to devour me.

"Do you know the damage you have caused? Especially for your *cousin*? Phoebe is the only lady in my brother's family that is of marrying age, and you encourage her terrible habits by taking her to a club to *gamble*. It is already terrible enough that you are to be betrothed to a Monster, but because of the abominable conduct you have bestowed on your cousin, now she must attend as well."

My ears were ringing from the volume of his shouts, but I had become unbothered by his irate displays over the years.

I thought about the Monsters for a moment.

It had been at least fifty years since Monsters had become part of high society, many of which had riches that were more than our own.

The Fitzroys were one of the few last standing human-only families, and that was coming to an end now that Phoebe and I were being forced to the ball.

My choice to marry was being stripped from me, or else I would end up with nothing. Part of me hoped for the nothing, to be able to escape from the reputation that chased me.

Your duty, I reminded myself bitterly.

"I know that you prefer men," the Duke said. "I have never judged you for that, Ezra. I don't even care that you will be betrothed to a Monster. I just want to see you finally settling down and parting ways with these vexing habits of yours that cause harm to us all. I was once a young man too. I chased lords and ladies alike before meeting your mother."

His honesty chilled me for a moment, and I released a breath, stiffening my jaw. "I don't want this life," I whispered. "I don't want to be you. I saw the letter about the Ball, and yes, I was going to ignore the bidding of Her Majesty the Queen. In fact, I meant to burn that damned letter. But I see how that was a mistake."

"It was a mistake," he grumbled, finally relaxing. "To even think you have a choice to disobey the Queen. I only want what is best for you. You may do your best to vex me, but one day I will be in my grave. Then and only then will I allow you to make jest of me, boy. Until then, you do as I command, willingly."

Willingly.

Without protest.

My father wanted me to be as submissive as my step-mother, Duchess Helen Fitzroy.

My father pulled the letter I had left at my home from his waistcoat, unfolding the paper. I glared at it, regretting my carelessness with it this morning.

"Dear Mister Ezra Fitzroy, On account of the slanderous rumors revealing your ungentlemanly persona and the ill-gotten disgrace of the Fitzroy name, Her Majesty is compelled to deem the Season bequeathed to you a failure. Henceforth, in order to restore your and your family's name, you are hereby ordered to attend the Monsters Ball by Her Majesty our Queen."

My father folded the note abruptly, seething once again at the reminder of my scandalous exploits.

"Even Her Majesty is aware of your disgrace. This letter alone is damning, a reprehensible mark on the family name. You are a despicable son, and an even more disgraceful Fitzroy."

His words lingered, settling over the two of us.

I ignored everything he had just said, pretending his words had been lined with daisies instead of daggers.

Silence fell, only interrupted by the jostling of our carriage and the clomp of the horses' hooves. The sounds of the city echoed around us, a blanket of comfort surrounding me.

"Where are we going?" I asked.

"To *our* home," he sighed as if it should have been the most obvious.

His home, not mine. The extravagant house that he spoke of was the one he had moved into with his family, a large house that sat in the most prized district of Westminster. Mayfair was surrounded by the lavish parkland of Green and Hyde Park. Balconies decorated the front, allowing one to sit and watch the sun glitter over the trees and flowers, the manmade reservoir, and the sculptures my father had ensured ornamented his stead. The terraces were always littered with the pastel ruffles of the young ladies and society mothers that enjoy lounging with his young Duchess, and their rambunctious children that ran around with my younger siblings.

The house was never quiet. At least once a month, there would be a ball or party hosted. It was the expectation that when I took over for my father, my partner would host such lively events for the ton as well.

I much preferred my home in the heart of the Pimlico, the one that I had grown up in before it had become fashionable to live in Mayfair. I much preferred being closer to the city, the sounds of London never dying even well into the lamp-lit night. I preferred the sounds of drunken laughter as people left the pubs to the false ones of the chits and dandies that were the lifeblood of high society.

It was never dark in the heart of London, despite the

stars never making an appearance, yet I much preferred my effervescent abode to the Duke's hypocritical overtures of aristocracy that he had built the Mayfair house on.

One day, I told myself, one day I would move far from London. As much as I cherished this city, there was a darkness to it that haunted me. From the expectations of being the son of a duke, to the knowledge that this was where my mother had died years ago—I wanted to leave it all behind.

New Fitzroy Manor. I leaned to the side, peeking through the window to see that we were indeed headed there.

"You will be home until tomorrow night," my father stated. "Your clothes have been fetched, and you will be outfitted in the finest fabrics. I have a tailor that will be visiting on the morrow after breakfast. Tomorrow, you will meet your betrothed. You will court them. You will ask for their hand in marriage. We will have a wedding almost immediately as soon as they are chosen. It will be a momentous occasion, one that will solidify your name into the minds and on the tongues of all of London's assemblage. It will be your last season as an eligible bachelor. You will settle down, inherit more responsibility, and turn away from this wretched behavior that has labeled you as a rake."

It seemed that I now had no choice but to concede.

"If you refuse or make a spectacle of yourself at the Monster's Ball tomorrow, you will be disowned as a Fitzroy. You will be nameless, penniless, and you will become a man no one in this fine city will want to know. I will ensure no respectable establishment nor person will hire you. It will be as if you have died. I am aware of your other bank accounts. I am aware of your plans to try and escape to the country. This dream of living without your duty is just that —a dream. One that will become a hellish nightmare if you choose to disobey. Do you understand, Ezra?"

My stomach turned sour, the blood draining from my face.

Had I been a fool this entire time?

"Yes, father," I said tonelessly.

I turned my attention to look outside of the carriage, desolately watching the world pass by me.

I took a deep breath, steadying myself and accepting my fate.

The Monster's Ball would be the end of my era of freedom.

A Quadrille

P an

The Monster's Ball is the most anticipated event of the Season, this author dares to say, even for the Crown. A most purposeful expedient and the swan song for the failed ladies of the Season and the eligible lords that have yet to be matched. To this author's surprise, the Crown has mandated the presence of one said Satyr King, making us wonder if the distinguished royal has fallen from grace or if he merely searches for a suitable mate amongst London's ton. Has the monster crown finally decided that a lowly human might be an acceptable mark, or is there another reason for his sudden desperation? Could it be that his brother threatens to rise to power? Soon, our High Society will discover his true intentions, starting with the outcome of the Monster's Ball.

— Lady Grey, The High Tea.

"MY GODS," I SAID, LAUGHING AS I RIPPED THE GOSSIP RAG IN half. "This author is simply fantastic. I have never felt such a stirring before! I would feel outraged if it weren't so delightful."

"The High Tea is known to be controversial, Your Majesty. I suggest you do your best to ignore such distasteful slander," Ambrose said, grimacing as I tossed the paper to the floor of our carriage.

Ambrose was the son of a well-known duke and was a very renowned monster of machinery. He had long horns, dusty purple skin, and broad shoulders. There had been a time when I had fancied him, but had found myself enjoying his companionship much more than the thought of an occasional amorous congress. I had done my best to surround myself with individuals that prized me for more than my status, and Ambrose was one of them.

Ambrose would have much preferred to be back in his home at Haverhorn Manor tinkering away at his devices than in a carriage with his King, but here we were regardless. The poor bastard had been summoned by Lottie, and who was he to deny Her Majesty?

"Indeed," I said, raising a brow. "You look positively morose, my friend. Is my company so distasteful?"

"Never, Your Majesty," Ambrose sighed. "I simply do not wish to wed. I don't suppose you could talk to Her Majesty..."

"No, she would have my head for disagreeing with her on such a matter. She certainly enjoys forcing eligible bachelors out onto the open range, watching mamas pounce and bestow their offspring on such unwilling lords. As for being wed, I do not either," I said, wondering how my life would

change after tonight. "I much prefer to have my lovers. But...
if settling down is what I must do to keep my crown, then so
be it."

"Well, you are a King, being faithful is..."

"I will be faithful to whomever I choose," I said
staunchly, feeling a mild prick at my pride. "If I am lucky, I
will meet my fated mate. I've seen what that can do to even
the most rakish of monsters."

Mayhap my luck would change. At least, I hoped it to be
true, but perhaps such an engagement was no more than a
Banbury tale.

"Fated mate," Ambrose scoffed. "I am unsure that I
believe in such a myth."

"I have seen it so," I said, looking out of our carriage as
London passed us by.

It had been three days since I had arrived to my Mayfair
residence, and I had found myself settling in nicely. The
human cities were so much more different than those of my
lands, but I enjoyed their liveliness thoroughly.

What I didn't enjoy was dressing like a fop in the humid
June heat. I also did not enjoy the stench that wafted to the
west side of the city, and found it to be dismal outside of the
ton's pretty gardens.

I would take my lands over the abysmal poverty I saw,
and over the hatred that burned in most of the Town's eyes
when they saw a coach such as mine.

Still, it was not my kingdom. My world, although
connected to London, was far different, and I much
preferred it that way.

"Perhaps this is the last time we sit together unwed, dear
Ambrose," I sighed.

"Perhaps," Ambrose said, staring out the window.

A comfortable silence settled over us, but I refused to

allow myself to feel anything negative. Tonight would be one I would never forget, and I prayed to the old gods that they would finally give me the mate I had been wanting for so long.

Our coach slowed as we turned, the sound of the horses' hooves echoing on stone as they carried us up the long drive to the Lady's glorious home. Other coaches moved slowly in front of us as they stopped before the grand entrance and released their guests, the gowns of young ladies and waist-coats of eligible lords gleaming in the light of the setting sun. The air was sticky with heat, but even so, I found myself thinking of what lay ahead.

Lit lamps illuminated the abode, their small flames flickering as a light breeze picked up. Our carriage slowed to a halt and I waited as our footman came to the carriage door and opened it, placing a stool below.

Ambrose waited but I held out my hand. "Go on," I urged.

He nodded, his expression growing more and more morose as every second went by. He got out of the carriage and then waited to the side as I followed.

My hooves hit the ground, and I adjusted my clothing. I was a King, but I refused to dress in the manner that Queen Charlotte and the Prince Regent did, and I was able to get away with doing so because...Well, I *was* a King.

I wore a waistcoat, one that fit my body well. It was a deep purple with gold embellishments. Beneath it, I wore a vest and then my cravat. My cravat was always my favorite piece of whatever attire I chose to wear, and I had slowly gathered as they came into fashion. I wore breeches that stopped at my knees, allowing the rest of my satyr body to be exposed.

Everyone before me immediately curtsied, followed by the flutter of '*Your Majestys*'.

"Shall we?" I asked, leading the way.

Humans and monsters alike parted for me as I went up the stairs and to the grand entrance. I ignored the continued curtsies and acknowledgements, now wanting to be in the midst of everything that was happening. I wanted to see the dancers, the musicians, the lords and ladies. Specifically the lords.

Would I meet my mate tonight or was it just a fool's hope?

Even after being alive for so long, I never found myself jaded but at the prospect of my fated mate...or rather, the disillusion of a prospect, I found my steadfast resolve wavering.

I turned, pausing to give Ambrose a look. "Well, my friend. Good luck to us both."

"Good luck indeed, Your Majesty."

We entered the ballroom and were met with the sound of lively music. The lilt of violins drifted through, playing the type of music that often put me to sleep.

As I moved inside, eyes fell on me, and I availed the momentary interruption caused by the curiosity to peruse the market in return.

Ladies and lords, monsters and humans alike looked on at me with eager anticipation, wondering if they would be my chosen.

For a brief moment, I felt the rise of fear again. If I couldn't find a match, then my brother would challenge my crown. It had long been tradition that our ruler had a mate, and I had been living for so long without one beside me. Not that I needed one...but even monsters had their traditions that could not be simply ignored. Monsters wanted their King to have a mate, which would in turn be a symbol of hope they could emulate.

"Ambrose, I do think that I am..." I drifted off, turning to realize that Ambrose and I had already been lost from each other.

"Good evening, Your Majesty."

Ah blazes, the mamas had found me. They were worse than sirens, waiting to feast on any eligible soul that had wandered into their waters.

"Your Majesty! I'd like to introduce you to my daughter, Lady Beaumont."

"My King! I'd like to introduce you to my son, Lord Grant."

Too soon, I was barraged with an avalanche of introductory marital prospects and completely surrounded by textured pastels of dresses.

Still, I looked on, grazing the ballroom. There were pillars that dripped with flowers, strings of lanterns waving above our heads. I could see the horns of other creatures here and there, catching the sway of a tail or claws occasionally mixed in with humans.

I was merely a few steps past the entrance, having not even made it to the center of the grand room. I could see the dance floor, and couples trading partners, shuffling like a pretty deck of cards as the music carried them.

My gaze stopped on one lord, a man that clung to the edges of the festivities, and in a similar situation as me. He was surrounded by a ravenous group of mamas, all thrusting their children on him. He looked angry about it though, unlike me who found this type of attention to be fun.

I could see the vein popping in his forehead from here.

I found myself smirking, unable to take my eyes from him.

"Pardon me," I said, raising my voice loud enough to command attention. "There appears to be someone in need of me."

Everyone parted for me as I went towards the man who needed rescuing, eyes wide as I crossed the floor, ignoring the curtsies and hails.

"Make way," I said, my voice immediately parting the circle around him.

His eyes widened for a moment, his expression turning even angrier as I approached him. Our gazes locked, his dark brown eyes burning as if they held the flames of his soul trapped within them. His hair was a light golden brown, soft waves that stopped at his shoulders. His jaw ticked, his brows drawing together.

"Your Majesty," he said.

"What is your name?" I asked.

"Ezra Fitzroy the Third, Sir," he answered, his words edged with spite.

Such an angry little buck.

I held out my hand, offering it to him. He wavered for a moment, his expression becoming unreadable. "I should like to dance with you, if you so desire," I said.

"My card is full," he said.

"Oh?" I asked, looking around us. Eyes feasted on our exchange, whispers and murmurs surrounding us. "Hmm. Then, I shall replace whomever is on that list then. There is a calling for a quadrille, and I would like to participate with you at my side, Lord Fitzroy."

He glared for a moment, and I watched as he regained his composure in the blink of an eye.

I liked vexing him, I realized. It was more fun than I

should have allowed.

"I am a King," I reminded him.

"Yes, Your Majesty," he all but spat out.

His hands were gloved, but as he slid his palm into mine, I felt a thrill run through me. We stared at each other, my breath hitching for a moment.

"Excellent. Come," I said, pulling him away from the crowd and towards the dance floor.

There were three other couples waiting, and to my surprise, Ambrose was amongst the mix. I raised a brow, our gazes meeting for a moment.

I tucked young Ezra's arm with mine, pulling him closer. "I needed to be rescued, as did you. Thank you," I offered.

"I was perfectly fine," he quipped.

"Ah yes, you looked more than," I teased, stealing another glance at him.

Never had someone looked so miserable in my presence unless they had done something worthy of punishment.

We joined the other couples on the dance floor, and I put him into the position that ladies typically took. He stiffened immediately, letting out a soft growl as he was faced with the circumstances. We were the only couple made of two men, but no one paid much attention to that matter.

"Lord Fitzroy," I said. "Do you not know this dance?"

"I do," he answered. "Typically from the other position."

"Ah, I see. Well, this will be fun for you then," I said.

Ambrose's eyes left me and fixed on one of the other couples, a pretty woman in a pastel pink dress and the monster that stood next to her, an intimidating sight indeed for Lord Benedict Balfour was a gargoyle..

"My King," Lord Balfour said. "It is an honour to be on the dance floor with you."

The other couple also curtsied, offering similar words.

"Indeed," I said, grinning. "This will be most fun for us all!"

The lady in the pastel dress offered a wide smile, charming us all. Ezra also looked at her, his expression immediately softening.

"Dear Cousin," Ezra said, his tone completely different now that he was with someone familiar. "You seem to have been trapped by fate as well."

She only gave him a pleasant smile, her eyes meeting his. "If fate has designs for me to be in the company of Lord Balfour, then perhaps fate is kind after all."

Ambrose cleared his throat and I glanced over at him, raising a brow at his out of character display. In fact, that he had even graced the dance floor was not commonplace for him.

Interesting. My attention went back to Ezra's cousin, and upon further scrutiny, I could see the resemblance now.

"Lady Fitzroy," Lord Balfour said. "You honour me with such words."

Ezra glowered at Lord Balfour. "Oh, Lord Balfour, I do think my cousin is being overly generous."

Lady Fitzroy's eyes became daggers, further proof that perhaps it ran in the Fitzroy family to be both fierce and polite.

The cousins seemed to have a silent exchange, one that was further telling that they indeed belonged to the same family. Only this lady wore a smile and radiated a buzz of excitement that was almost contagious, whereas Ezra was nothing but sullen.

The music began and I cracked a grin of my own as Ezra and I were forced to the center, both of us trotting to the middle before bouncing back, the next two people taking the next turn.

22

The next set took their turn, Lady Fitzroy and the lord whose name I had forgotten, doing a twirl before returning. Next was Ezra and one of the ladies, but then he returned to my side.

This human. I enjoyed seeing his temple throb and hearing his voice drop to a low growl. He was beginning to seethe with anger, all while being so painfully obvious that he wanted more.

He would be a challenge.

"You have made a poor choice to dance with me," Ezra mumbled at my side as we watched the others.

"I think not," I said, amused.

I returned to the center, my hooves clacking against the floor before I came back to him. Our bodies pressed against one another's, the warmth of him against me making me feel things I had never felt before. I slid one of my hands to his waist briefly, feeling his taut muscles through his waistcoat.

"Do you doubt my ability to make choices, Lord Fitzroy?"

We broke apart, the music and conversation swirling around us. The crowd watched with delight as those in the quadrille danced with the Satyr King. Perhaps, I would even end up in The High Tea again, the thought bringing an amusing smile to my face

Ezra looked up at me as we returned to each other once again, his gaze sharp. "I am a scoundrel."

He said it with such conviction, the same way I said 'I am a King'. It was with an absolute truth, his words holding his belief.

"And?"

His expression wavered, before he trotted to the center, doing a twirl with Ambrose before coming back.

23

"Your poker face must be shite," I chuckled under my breath.

"It is not," he growled.

"Are you certain?" I asked. "Because everyone in the room right now knows that you are unyielding to your King, which is almost damaging to my image, I dare say."

"And what image is that, Your Majesty?" he asked as I pulled him close again.

The two of us had fallen into the dance, moving together like autumn leaves caught in a gust of wind. I pulled him as close as possible without causing a scandal, and growled into his ear.

"The image of a King capable of seducing even a scoundrel."

He scoffed as I let go of him, and to both my shock and delight, the bastard walked right off the floor. There was a symphony of gasps, but I only smiled, offering the rest of the dance to the nearest couple before following after him.

Only a fool would dare embarrass a King like this, and yet, I wasn't angry.

My heart thrashed in my chest, my blood running hot, but it wasn't ire that made my gaze follow him. It was something much more dangerous, much more enthralling.

A human had never made me feel this way.

Hell, not even a monster had.

I wanted him, and I decided in that very moment that I would have him.

I thought about him in my arms again, even as he pushed through the gathered crowd. I could hear him growling at the ton to make way, and allow him his escape.

Running from me. A monster. The Satyr King.

He wouldn't escape.

No.

I wouldn't allow it to happen.

Out of every creature in attendance tonight, he was the only one that I had designs for.

The feeling settled into my gut, the knowledge that fate had finally chosen to give me what I had waited for all along.

A mate.

Ezra Fitzroy III, a scoundrel son of a duke, was to be my mate.

Scandalous Duel

⁌⁌⁌

Ezra

I BROKE THROUGH THE DOUBLE DOORS, AND OUT INTO THE humid evening. I ignored the watchful eyes following me, and instead headed straight into the garden outside of the widowed Countess of Stalbridge's grand home.

I couldn't stand this miserable occasion for another moment. I would scale the wall at the edge of the property and take off into the night. No one would know any better, being that they were occupied with the fancies of the drum. To think that I was forced to attend the ball, to be such a spectacle, made me furious. The Queen was too desperate to marry us off.

My thoughts spun, my rage growing hotter and hotter.

The damned Satyr King had made me into a cork-brained zany. A laughing stock. As if enough eyes weren't already on me, he had brought even more attention by forcing me to dance with him.

What in the heavens and hells was the Satyr King wanting anyways?

I hated him, and I hated that there was this feeling clawing at my chest since the moment our hands had touched. The devil himself must have chosen me as the heir of all misfortune, for to feel such....baffling things for a monster and cock-sure King was unacceptable.

I hated the royal family and the society they had created. Women were often looked on as nothing more than breeding stock, and the thorough education of both sexes was frowned upon. This King was part of a grander problem, one that I lived in defiance of.

I plunged into the darkness and paused, realizing that the Stalbridge gardens had changed since I had last been in them. In fact, I was now in a maze.

My anger continued as I made my way through arcs of leaves, the floral scents following me.

"Lord Fitzroy!"

"Fiend seize it," I hissed, glancing back over my shoulder.

The Satyr King had followed me into the gardens.

I moved faster, going through an opening that revealed a small gazebo with a fountain at the center. Moonlight reflected off the dripping water as I passed it, my boots stomping over the ground.

"Lord Fitzroy," he growled.

A hand reached out and grabbed hold of me, and I immediately spun, shoving him back. He was faster and stronger than I had expected, though, and in one swift motion I found myself pinned against one of the gazebo pillars, captive of a monster I wanted nothing to do with.

Our breaths came out in harsh pants, but his eyes didn't burn with anger like I imagined mine did.

"Unhand me," I sneered.

"No," he said, his lips tugging into a devious smirk. "Be still, little buck."

"King or not, I will box you," I said, my heart pounding in my chest.

His gaze slid over me, his horns glinting in the moonlight. I could hear the sounds of the party in the distance, but it was as if we were worlds away. I found myself drawn into his eyes, my muscles unwillingly losing their tension.

I yielded to no one, but here I was, giving into him.

"Tell me," he whispered. "Why is it that you hate the ton so much?"

"Because...this society is nothing but a facade," I growled. "I am the son of a duke, and yet I am forced to attend this terrible place simply because I prefer to spend my time with those lower than me in rank and have not found someone to wed. Anyone who does not fit in with the Queen is to be crammed into her little box of diamonds, forced to be sharpened and shined just like every other one. No matter if you are an emerald or a ruby."

"I see," he said, amused.

He was much taller than me, I realized. Taller, and his shoulders were broader. Not to mention that his legs were covered in tawny fur and ended in hooves, with ebony horns protruding from his golden locks. He was ageless, but his eyes sparkled with an excitement that I could not fathom.

"Am I a game to you, Sir?" I seethed.

"No. Far from it," he said, leaning in closer.

I swallowed hard, all of my worries melting away. I was drawn further into him, into the way he held me still, to the scent of him. He was a King, and yet that didn't cross my mind at that very moment.

All I could think of was how my cock was starting to harden, my breeches feeling tight, and my head spinning with the thrill of wanting someone.

He leaned closer, his lips hovering above mine.

"This is inappropriate, my King," I whispered, my voice husky. "If someone found us this way, it would surely cause a scandal."

"It could," he murmured, almost touching me. "Tell me no again, little buck."

Little buck. I should have been offended by being called such a thing, but I found that my blood only ran hotter.

"I won't tell you no," I said.

"Then unbutton your breeches and show me what is straining within them for my touch already, little buck."

Heat spread through me, and for once in my life, I was at a loss for words. I had never been in this position— flustered and unsure in equal measure.

Yet, I found my hands falling to my pants as I popped three of the buttons and then the rest.

"Satyr King—"

"Call me Pan," he corrected, running the back of his hand over my jaw as I let my pants fall, my cock springing free.

Pan's hand immediately took my shaft, gripping me firmly. I let out a helpless groan, leaning back against the gazebo column that now prevented me from swooning like a chit. Pleasure had me in its binds, my willpower crumbling beneath his touch.

"Such a thick sword," he teased. "I heard there are some creatures who can swallow swords without being cut."

"Oh?" I asked, shuddering as he began to stroke me.

"Yes," he said. "Are you one of those creatures, Lord Fitzroy?"

"Yes," I grunted. I breathed out a curse, my head falling back as he moved his hand faster. A monster king was stroking my cock, and driving me towards a cliff of pleasure I could not escape. "Call me Ezra."

"Ezra," Pan said softly, pulling his hand free. He leaned forward, his expression still open and amiable, but his words dark and commanding. "Get on your knees for me, Ezra."

It was almost gentle in the way he spoke, but I immediately obeyed. It was as if I were nothing more than a puppet, my knees buckling. I realized I was kneeling in a position of supplication before my King, my cock throbbing with need as I gazed up at him.

Pan swept his waistcoat back, undoing the buttons of his breeches. I watched as his long fingers undid button after button, and then the fabric slid down, revealing a cock unlike any I had ever seen in my life.

I gasped, gawking at him. His shaft was long and thick, and bright orange with a tapered head. At the very base, there was a bulbous protrusion, a knot, which was also something I had never seen before.

"What do you think, little buck?"

"Magnificent," I whispered reverently, reaching up.

Pan took my hand, tugging my glove off. His gaze held mine, the simmering heat of our exchange making me forget that I was supposed to hate this creature with every fiber of my being.

"Open your mouth wide, little buck," he whispered.

I opened my mouth as he brought my hand to his cock, allowing me to guide the head. I let out a soft grunt, sinking into this feeling of submission like I was born to be here.

All of my interactions, all of the men that I had been with, none of them had dared to ever put me on my knees and make me suck their cock.

Especially not a monster cock.

"Good boy," he whispered, his hips giving a gentle jerk.

I grunted as the head of his cock slid between my lips, his precum overcoming my tastes. I groaned as his sweet and tart taste filled my mouth, my mind swirling and on edge with the notion of being caught. If we were caught...

"Suck, little buck," he commanded.

All of the worrisome thoughts plaguing me drifted away as I began to move my mouth back and forth, sucking him. I gripped his shaft, submitting completely to this monster.

His fingers curled into my hair, gripping me as he began to thrust. The head of his shaft hit the back of my throat, but I only took him deeper.

Pan cursed, his breaths becoming ragged. Tears began to roll down my cheeks as I lost myself to him, my muscles relaxing as he used my throat and mouth. Over and over again, the feeling of his cock sliding in and out.

I raked my nails down his thighs, gripping the fur there. He let out a sudden cry, giving one final harsh thrust as his seed spilled.

I swallowed every drop, the heat rushing down my throat. He slowly pulled free.

My head was spinning, and I found myself licking my lips where stray drops of his cum were. He tasted incredible.

"Gods," Pan gasped, his chest heaving.

He offered me a hand, pulling me to a stand. My cock strained now, painfully hard.

"I suppose I should return the favor," Pan chuckled.

I was about to respond, when a couple of gasps echoed through the garden.

"Good heavens!! That's the scoundrel!"

"He has taken advantage of the Satyr King!"

I felt my blood run cold, my head whipping around to see that we had been found.

We had been caught.

Oh no. No, no, no.

Pan let out a small chuckle, which enraged me. I turned back around, reaching out to backhand him. Pan merely stepped back, my hand missing him completely.

"How dare you," I growled. "This will *ruin* me."

"Button your breeches," Pan said quickly.

He had already done so, looking much more presentable than me. I let out a curse, making myself presentable as more people began to gather.

Vulturous gazes picked us apart, but Pan stepped forward.

"My good humans and monsters, what you have seen here is merely a heated exchange between a King and his betrothed. Move along now, I command it."

There was an eruption of murmurs, but I could barely hear a damn thing over the rushing of my blood, my world going topsy turvy.

"Go!" Pan barked.

Betrothed.

The gathered crowd scattered, but it was too late.

The damage had been done.

I was officially ruined.

Or...I had just ruined a King.

A KING.

I leaned against the pillar, feeling faintish.

"This is... this is a nightmare," I whispered. "The ton will eat us alive. Eat me alive. My father...Fuck. No one will marry me."

"I will," Pan said. "I mean. I am. Now, come, we must go smooth over the rumors."

He reached for me, but I slapped his hand away. "You fucking fool!"

Pan raised a brow. "Such harsh language."

I let out a growl, ready to fight, but none other than my cousin emerged from the gardens. William. Followed by a monster fellow I'd seen on the dance floor earlier.

"Ezra," he growled, coming up to me. "What in the seven hells is going on? I just heard you *ruined* a King."

"He did," Pan said, grinning. "Can't say I've cum that hard in at least a century."

William made a noise.

"My King, we must go."

"But I'm just now having fun, Ambrose. And what happened to the Fitzroy girl, did you speak to her?"

"I'm engaged to her," Ambrose said.

Pan stared at him in baffled consternation for a moment, as did I.

Phoebe?

Phoebe was engaged?

"Close your gaping mouth, cousin," William said. "Even wild beasts can be tamed."

"Did you just call your sister a beast?"

"Well. Good work then," Pan said, grinning. "And I, too, am now engaged. This Ball was a splendid idea, I'm quite glad Her Majesty took up the idea."

"We are not engaged!" I burst out.

Pan waved his hand, ignoring me. He looked at William. "I suppose I should tell you this! But we shall have a wonderful proposal dinner so that I may meet the family.

All will be invited! Tomorrow night. Since this is such a scandalous engagement, we'll need to act fast to maintain our reputations. Good thing the Archbishop owes me a favor. You see, he likes nymphs in his bed and well... Ah, you didn't hear that from me. Now, you, my buck." Pan turned to look at me, his grin reminding me of the very devil himself. "I shall see you tomorrow, my Prince. We'll have to halt our relations until our wedding night, but I assure you, it will be here before you know it."

Before I could answer, Pan gave a short bow, and then sauntered off with my cousin's fiancé.

"Well," William said, watching as they went. "I am unsure of what to say, cousin, except at least one of you is happy."

"I'm going to murder him," I scoffed.

"Why? He is the answer to all of your problems."

"No. He is the reason for all of them! The whole ton will believe I ruined him, when he was in fact the one to come on to me!"

William winced. "Apologies, cousin, but it seems this is the hand fate has dealt you."

I let out a low growl and then let my head fall back, glaring up at the starry sky.

I had never been one to let a bad hand stop me from winning.

A Proper Proposal Dinner

❧

P^{an}

"WE MUST BRING OUT THE FINEST LINENS AND SILVERWARE," I
said.

"And what of flowers, my King? Do you approve of
peonies or—"

"I want fresh peonies and lavender," I said. "I want them
to match perfectly with the linens. And please, these are
humans, so I suppose we should also have lamb and duck."

My servants nodded, immediately leaving to tackle their
duties. I turned around, surveying the floor of the entry to
my Westminster estate.

"No, no, no," I said, looking up with a gasp. "There are
scuff marks on the floor!"

"We will make sure they are gone, my King," Bernard
said. "This will be the most perfect proposal dinner to ever
be had."

"It has to be!" I exclaimed. "I want my dearly beloved to know that he is in capable hands. While I may have rushed this, it is only because I was so sure he was the one."

It was true. What I felt when seeing Ezra turned every passionate embrace I had over the last few centuries to dust. His touch alone had set my heart on fire, his lips taking me to the very gates of heaven.

Compromising ourselves had been scandalous, sure, but I had never been one to care for the humans' rules. I had wanted him, so I had taken him. Now, he would be my prince, and my issue with my dear brother would be solved.

The Monster's Ball had gone exactly to plan. Last night had been a success, in more ways than I had thought possible. I had found my fated mate, and was desperate to have him at my side at once.

I reached into my pocket, pulling out my watch. "We have six hours to prepare," I said.

"It will be perfect, my King, I assure you," Bernard said.

I nodded, feeling myself relax. Bernard never broke a promise.

"Are you certain you want lamb and duck?" he asked. "You have never enjoyed eating such meats."

"I know, but the humans will. This dinner is for them."

Bernard nodded. "Right, Sir. I will update you once further preparations are underway."

"Thank you, Bernard," I said.

I watched as he went, breathing out a sigh. I looked around, feeling lonely again.

Would having Ezra rid me of that feeling?

What if we had children?

The ton's infamous scoundrel as a papa was enough to keep me grinning as I strolled through the house to the set of doors that went out into the small garden.

"My King, the latest paper has arrived."

I turned, plucking the High Tea off the silver platter one of my servants had readied for me.

"Have some tea brought, I will be out in the garden," I said.

"Yes, my King."

I headed for the fountain, taking a seat on the bench in front of it. A downy birch tree cast a shadow over me, the leaves softly rustling as a hot summer breeze lifted. It was still early in the day, but London was already wilting.

> *The Monster's Ball proved to be as exciting and scan-dalous as this author predicted. Of all the glamorous affairs of the evening, perhaps the most notable was that of Ezra Fitzroy the Third, the ton's scoundrel, being found in a most compromising liaison with none other than the Satyr King. The Scoundrel and the Satyr King have acted fast however, as a proposal dinner is to take place this very night.*

I stopped reading, surprised that the infamous Lady Grey hadn't ripped into the two of us. A light jabbing here, but nothing damaging. Perhaps the swift proposal dinner had done exactly what I had intended.

"My King. I have your tea, and the Archbishop has arrived."

"Oh good," I said. "Bring him out here."

They set my tea on a small table whilst another servant went to fetch the Archbishop.

I heard him grumbling before he arrived. I lifted my tea cup, pinky up, taking a sip right as he arrived, flustered and red in the face. I hoped that meant he had seen all the erotic statues in my garden. They were difficult to miss.

"John," I said, giving him a smirk. "Take a seat."

"My King, my apologies, but I cannot stay long. I have many duties to attend to—"

"I said *sit*, John," I said, my voice firm.

He paled before immediately taking a seat on the bench next to me with a labored breath. "It's too hot today, and the city reeks of mixed odours."

"It does," I agreed. "I need a favor. I have found my fated mate and thus require a special marriage license. Today. Within a few hours actually."

"Today?!"

"Yes," I said, looking up at him. I took another sip of my tea, not caring that I was making him uncomfortable. "I need one for Ezra Fitzroy the Third and myself."

"I will need his word—"

"You will get me the license today, John."

"But— but—"

I set my cup of tea down and leaned forward, grinning. "Little Archbishop. I am a King. I require this. Do you understand? Now, go. I will have someone fetch the certificate from you later today."

I stood up, taking my cup of tea, and strolled off before he could argue.

Now, everything was in order. This evening, we would have our matrimonial festivities, and all would be well. I would be wed, my crown secure, and my mate satiated.

Everything would be perfect.

THE SCOUNDREL AND THE SATYR KING

"THIS IS NOT PERFECT," I WHISPERED, HORRIFIED AS I watched Ezra's family carriages arrive. I looked up at Ambrose, feeling a moment of panic. "Is everything ready?"

"Everything is, my King."

I had dragged him to my proposal dinner, mostly because I knew his betrothed would be here, and because I needed another monster around and a companion.

"Are you certain? Are we sure? Oh goodness, I am feeling faint. As if it matters what these humans think."

"Everything is more than perfect," Ambrose said softly, trying to calm me. "Just pertinent nerves, my King. Also, you'll be pleased to know that your special license has arrived. All is well."

I nodded, taking a deep breath, stealing myself. I'd spent the last hour working myself up, concerned over trivial matters in order to distract from my blooming panic.

I was realizing more and more that I really did want Ezra to be impressed.

I'd even had every bed aside from mine taken out of the house.

"How are you feeling?" I asked Ambrose.

He made a face, one that was indiscernible. "I'm fine."

"Excellent, so we feel the same then. Both liars. Let's go meet them."

The doors to my home were opened for me and I stepped outside, going down the steps with Bernard and several others following.

The door to the carriage opened, and out stepped a much older and crankier version of Ezra. His sharp eyes regarded me with keen appraisal for a moment, and then he gave a slight bow.

"Your Majesty," he said. "I am John Fitzroy II, Duke of Devonshire. This is my wife, Duchess Helen Fitzroy." He held out his hand, helping a lady out of the carriage that certainly bore no relation to Ezra.

"Your Majesty," she said, curtseying. "It is our honour to meet you. To think that you would be compromised by Ezra, it is—"

John cut her off, clearing his throat. "I hope it is okay, but I brought my brother's family with me as well."

"That's perfectly acceptable," I said. "And where is Ezra?"

"He..." John drifted off, wincing. "He will be along shortly. He ran into an issue with his clothing, so we are having one of our servants help him."

Ah. That was a lie.

I narrowed my eyes, but let it go.

I watched as two children came out of the carriage, a boy and a girl that were brimming with excitement. I smiled at them, holding out my hand.

"Hello, younglings," I chuckled.

The girl took my hand, her cheeks bright pink. "Your Majesty. My name is Elizabeth," she said, curtseying.

"Good name. And you, good sir?" I asked, offering the young boy my hand next. He took it, swinging it wildly.

"John," he said, grinning.

Children were always so rambunctious, and it amused me.

"Stop behaving like a fool," older John hissed, rapping his cane out.

I let go of his hand, scowling. "They are perfectly fine, my Lord, I assure you."

The other carriage door opened, and out came a man who must have been John's brother, followed by his son William, and then daughter Phoebe.

I stole a glance at Ambrose, watching as he went to greet them. Our group closed in, chatter ringing the air, and yet...

Ezra was missing.

Had he stood me up? At our own proposal dinner?

The thought both amused me and humiliated me.

The sound of hooves on stone echoed and I looked up, surprised to see the devil himself running up on his horse. I watched as he slowed his mount, his caramel hair ruffled by a breeze. He was wearing a black waistcoat and a charming top hat, gloves, and breeches that I wanted to tear off his body.

I thought about last night, and found that my heart began to beat faster. Heat rushed through me, the feeling of his mouth taking my cock haunting me.

He avoided my gaze as he hopped off, handing the reins to one of the servants.

"Oh, what a fine horse," Ambrose said.

"Don't admire the horse, admire your bride to be," I teased, giving him a friendly jab.

I moved through the crowd, going to meet Ezra. He paused, looking up at me. There was still anger there, perhaps a little hurt as well.

I frowned. "Let us speak alone, before we continue with dinner," I said, offering him my hand.

He nodded, taking it.

"We shall return," I said, "the two of us must discuss some things before dinner. Feel free to explore the gardens."

"Shouldn't someone accompany you both?" his father asked with a frown.

"No, I think we are compromised enough that another delicate incident surely will not matter much more, and quite frankly—I don't care for human rules. We shall return shortly."

41

My words caused a gasp from Helen, whom I already didn't like. I ignored her, stealing Ezra away. I led him up the steps of my abode, and guided him into the library.

I shut the door behind us.

Ezra let out a long sigh, pulling his hand free. "I am not happy about this arrangement. You used me."

I winced, but didn't deny it. How did I explain that this was so much more than a means to an end for our situations?

"Ezra," I said, meeting his gaze. "What we felt last night was very real. I saw an opportunity, and I took it. I do have to be wed and find a mate."

"You are forcing me into this marriage."

"Society is," I said. "Besides. It could be worse. You could have ended up with someone who wasn't a King."

"I have no interest in being a Prince."

I crossed my arms, studying him. "Be honest with me. Do you want to be a Duke?"

Ezra's breath faltered, and he was silent for a moment. "No," he finally said. "I have never wanted to live up to nor receive my father's title."

"Right. Well, your *duties* as a Prince will now prevent you from taking on his business. He will need to pass it to young John."

"And what *duties* are those?"

"Whatever you want them to be," I said.

Ezra's eyes widened, realization finally dawning.

"You are no longer obliged to the Fitzroys. You may continue to gamble and drink and do as you wish. My only stipulation is that you may not be with anyone else sexually. You are mine, and belong to me, and me alone, in that way. The same can be said for me. I will partake in no carnal unions outside of our marriage bed. If there are orgies, I will simply watch."

"Orgies?" Ezra rasped.

"Oh yes. The Land of Essex is far different than London, little buck. I think you will find that the ways of my world are much more kind to someone like you than your own. You will live in a beautiful place, with all the riches you could ask for, and freedom."

"And my father can't say otherwise…"

"Correct."

Ezra leaned back against my desk, his shoulders relaxing. "This might…this might actually work to our favor."

I nodded, giving him a soft smile. "I hope so. I do like you."

"I hated you," Ezra said. "All last night. Up until this very moment, in fact. And I'm still not happy. I feel tricked. But… this might work."

"Well. Let's do our best," I said. "You have to convince your family you are meant to be with me, and I must convince my brother who may or may not show up."

Ezra nodded and seeing him agree made me happy. "We can convince them."

"Excellent," I said. "Then let us return to them and see if my dearest bastard of a brother has arrived."

Buring Revelations

E zra

"A TOAST," WILLIAM SAID, RAISING HIS GLASS. "TO THE NEW couples. May their marriages be filled with newly wedded bliss, and their proposals go smoothly for us all."

I shot him a dirty look, but raised my glass, sipping it. I let out a satisfied hum, giving my wine a second look. It had an extraordinary flavor.

The table in the dining room seated all eleven of us, only one seat empty for Pan's brother who had decided not to show.

My life had taken a complete turn since yesterday, and I didn't know what to think. One moment I had been less than inclined to be in Pan's presence, and in the next, I wanted nothing more than for his cock to be filling me over and over again. Furthermore, I found the prospect of being wedlocked to him... appealing.

I watched as my father and stepmother exchanged doubtful looks, already deeming Pan as lesser for accepting someone like me despite his kingly sovereignty. That infuriated me more than I could fathom—their endeavor to discreetly ridicule his worth as his association to me solidified.

"So," my father said, looking around the table. His eyes landed on Pan. "You are a King. A monster King."

"I am," Pan said, cocking his head. His lips tugged up, but he held back a grin. "And you are a duke. Since we are being observant."

I snorted and my father scoffed.

"This situation is very...problematic for a King, I would presume."

"Not at all," Pan said. "The ton do love a good scandal, and quite honestly, my life is far removed from here. I have a Kingdom to run, and being in the Queen's good graces allows me to do so without concern. But once Ezra and I are wed, we will leave for Essex where he will take on duties as a Prince."

My father's aghast expression pleased me. He sputtered, his brows shooting up. "Ezra is to take over the family business!"

"Yes, well. That's what little John is here for," Ezra chuckled, patting his head.

"I want my head to be pat," Elizabeth whined.

Pan leaned over and patted her head, making her laugh.

"Honestly, Uncle," Phoebe said. "Did you really think that Ezra marrying a *King* would give him time to take on the family business?"

"Phoebe," Uncle James warned, giving her a stern look.

"I am just saying," Phoebe sighed dramatically.

45

"I'm sure that your other son will be fine," Ambrose said, trying to smooth over everything with a calming voice.

"I didn't know Ezra would be this stupid, so I hadn't planned for this," my father said.

Pan's muscles stiffened and I looked up, surprise overtaking me at the malice filling his gaze upon hearing my father's words. It was like watching a playful lamb assume claws and fangs, and a very ravenous appetite.

"Ezra is quite the opposite of stupid, or else I would not be taking him as my mate," Pan said. "I would like to remind you that he is being wed to a King."

"Well, yes. But a monster. Your royal regard is not the same as ours."

"*Father*," I growled, feeling a streak of rage.

Pan let out a loud laugh, but the expression on Ambrose's face told me that perhaps my father was in danger, his self-pride advancing as the instrument of his ruin.

"The Duke is just jesting," Helen said, tugging on his arm. "Aren't you, dear?"

"Of course," he lied.

Pan reached for his wine glass, taking a measured sip. "It is funny to me that you think less of monsters, when monsters have been around for far longer than humans. We have been civilized a lot longer as well. Not to mention, I knew Lottie when she was just a babe. I knew Charles when he was just a boy, and when his father was just a boy. His father's father. In fact, I have watched this kingdom rise from the dirt, all while running mine. That is how long our royalty has been around. I have wealth that you cannot fathom. I have a life that you could never understand. And I have connections, far-reaching, that could end your dukedom tomorrow if I so pleased. I could call on the

Queen right now, and even as her advisor, you would be tossed out on your behind like nothing more than a bellboy. So, *Duke John*, I would caution you to mind your tongue when a King wants it so."

James cleared his throat loudly, giving his brother an exasperated look. Still, my father's gaze was pinned on Pan and Pan was holding it.

"All of that is to say, running a dukedom is now *beneath* my fiancé. Your stations will not be the same. He will be a prince, one that will be as loved as I am as a king."

"Well," my father said, glaring. He looked right at me, raising his glass. "I hope you are happy."

"I am," I said. "Very happy. Pan and I are meant to be together."

I could feel all eyes on me now, everyone staring at me like I was a ghost.

"It's true," I lied, looking over at Pan. I reached for his hand, giving him a fierce squeeze. "I am his, and he is mine."

"Yes," Pan said. "Which is why I took the liberty to secure a special license for us. We will be wed the morning of Sunday, three days from now, and Ezra will come with me to the land of Essex. Then you can forget all about us and be on your merry way."

We all stared at him in shock, even me.

Shite.

"And in the meantime, Ezra will be staying here at my Westminster home. I took the liberty of having my servants bring his belongings here."

What?

"Tomorrow morning, we will all promenade," Pan said excitedly. "And I will show off my new scoundrel of a fiancé to all of the Town. It will be spectacular."

. . .

THE REST OF THE DINNER HAD GONE BY QUICKLY, AND SOON I found myself standing next to my monstrous fiancé in the foyer of his home, surrounded by my belongings that had been retrieved from my home in Pimlico.

My temper was causing sweat to roll down the back of my neck, my muscles tense.

"You are a right bastard," I whispered, not sure what else to say.

Pan spread his arms wide, grinning. "We did it! They believed everything. This is what you wanted, right?"

"No, Pan, it is not!" I bellowed, my voice echoing through the hall.

Pan stepped forward, his hooves meeting my boots. He tipped my chin up, forcing me to look up at him.

"You said this marriage would help you, little buck."

"You are forcing me into this," I growled. "You went into my home and took my things! Without my permission!"

"I am a king. Of course I didn't go into your home. I had someone do it for me. Besides, I do believe your society would not be too happy to find the Satyr King in an area like Pimlico."

"You can kiss the very bottom of my boots," I hissed. "You are manipulative and commanding and a wolf in sheep's clothing!"

Pan gripped my jaw, drawing a shocked breath from me as he held me firmly. He let out a low growl, one that stirred my cock in a way that I found horrifying.

"I think it is time for us to rest," Pan said softly. "Come to bed, little buck, and perhaps you will feel better on the morrow."

"Yes, I'd like to see the chambers you're sticking me in," I bit out, yanking my face free.

Pan let out a mirthless chuckle. "Yes, let me show you."

I didn't like how pleased he sounded. Pan was far more formidable than I had expected. The Satyr King had not only manipulated me into this situation, but he had silenced my father—who was notably unsilenceable.

My heart began to pound in my chest as Pan turned, his hooves clacking against the marble floors as he went up the staircase. I could feel the watchful eyes of the servants as I followed Pan, feeling as though I was walking straight to my doom.

I scowled, my eyes focusing on Pan's ass as I followed him.

He had a tail.

My fiancé had a tail.

Good heavens, I was in over my head.

"It was quite cruel how we had to leave each other at the Ball," Pan said as he led me down a hall. "I desire more time with you."

I felt another flare of anger, followed by...by something else. Arousal.

I hadn't slept last night. No. I hadn't been able to after the events that had occurred, and I had spent my time cumming over and over again while hating Pan. He was toxic, a poison that had spilled over my life.

We went down the hall until we came to a grand set of doors. Two guards waited there, and opened them upon our approach, presenting what was most definitely Pan's chambers.

I followed Pan inside and the doors shut promptly behind us. I scowled, letting out a frustrated sigh.

The room was not quite as lavish as I had expected, but it was still ornate. A four poster bed sat at the center, the ceiling above us mirrored. The windows were draped with velvet burgundy curtains, lanterns casting shadows over the chairs and table that sat in front of a fireplace on the opposite end of the room. Then there was the adjoining bathing room, a pedestal sink next to the door. I could see the copper tubs from here.

Not one, but two.

Everything that belonged to Pan reminded me of a peacock, all of the colors drowning out the dull browns and grays of the world.

"These are your quarters."

"And now yours as well," Pan said, grinning. "Your bed is my bed, dear fiancé."

"Absolutely not," I growled. "I don't sleep next to my lovers, and certainly won't sleep next to you. We have already started so many rumors!"

"Then you will have to take to the floor, I'm afraid. I had the staff remove all the beds today besides this one that is. We have one bed."

"You *what*?" I hissed. "You are insane! Ludicrous!"

"Perhaps," Pan said, turning to smirk at me. "I want you, Ezra. Let me show you what it is really like to be with a King. You are so worried about what society will say, but they cannot touch you the same way anymore. Think about all the... *situations* that you have heard about with the King and Queen. And yet...society knows better than to challenge them. And I simply do not care. I want you, Ezra Fitzroy. I have been unable to rid you from my thoughts. You haunt my very monstrous being, little buck. Even breathing the same air as you makes my cock harden and my soul burn."

His words tore away my shields, my own voice faltering. How did I respond to him?

Pan stepped closer, the warmth of his body drawing me near.

"Tell me no," he whispered.

"I cannot," I murmured, shutting my eyes. I clung to the darkness for a moment, before opening them and meeting his gaze. "I cannot tell you no."

He turned me, walking me to the pedestal sink with the mirror.

I felt Pan's cock against the tight fabric of my pants, the hardness causing me to gasp. The damn Satyr King pressed me against the wash basin, his eyes gleaming in the mirror in front of us. He reached around, taking the steel straight razor and shaving soap that awaited there.

"Allow me," he said.

I wanted to argue. I wanted to fight this arrogant bastard and tell him, again, that I would never be wed to a monster like him. Instead, I allowed him to pluck the razor and soap, not fighting him.

His hand lifted, cupping my jaw and forcing my head to the side. The shaving soap was spread over my skin, and I swallowed hard as he held the blade aloft.

"Have you ever shaved a man's face?" I asked, glaring at him despite going very, very still.

"It has been a while," Pan said, his cock pulsing against me. "Be very still, darling, I would hate to hurt such a devilishly pretty face."

His fingers tightened, his hips thrusting harder against me, pinning me to the sink. He began to swipe the blade, clearing off a swathe of the soap.

He wiped it on the towel that was slung over the holder before placing it over my shoulder, and then started to shave me again.

I was nothing but a human plaything to this bastard. All of proper society said that *I* was the scoundrel, that I had no future because I was a rogue. But here was this king, a monster, a creature that I had no business being in the presence of—pinned me with his cock against my ass, and a razor at my throat.

"You, my King, are a brute," I whispered through still lips.

"I am not," Pan chuckled. "I am a perfect member of high society. Those below me worship me. I am friendly..." he said, swiping the blade against my face again, "...kind, loving, benevolent. A great person to have drinks with."

"You are a monster," I sneered. "One that I should have never agreed to wed. Scandal or not."

"Am I so terrible, little buck?" Pan asked, although he wore his lopsided grin again.

I never knew if he took anything I said seriously.

I studied him as he continued to shave me, my heart pounding in my chest as his cock continued to pulse against me. He was striking. His formidable horns curling from his shiny blonde hair. His searching blue eyes were unnaturally beautiful, always sparkling with mischief.

He shaved off the last of my stubble, cleaning the blade. He then leaned forward, his voice almost musical.

"Take these breeches off, Sir. I am shaving all of you."

"No," I said.

"Have you forgotten your station in this predicament?" Pan asked, smiling against my ear.

I wanted to hate him. Despise him for uttering such things to me. But, still, all of the blood pumping through my veins began to flow downwards, no matter how hard I tried to stop it.

"Remove your articles," Pan said, his voice a little more firm this time.

He took a step back, waiting ever so patiently. I leaned forward, my thoughts tumbling over each other as I tried to see a way out of this.

THE SCOUNDREL AND THE SATYR KING

I didn't want out of this, I realized.

I straightened, looking at Pan. His furred haunches were still clothed in tight pants that did little to hide his bulge. His silk shirt was open displaying his fierce chest that my lips had marked only last night.

"Have you bewitched me?" I asked.

"No, I have not. I am a Satyr, not a witch," Pan said, cocking his head to the side. "Come, you silly man. It is simply a shave. I will not give you my cock until you beg for it, even if it aches to be buried inside of you again."

My breath hitched and I turned, heat spreading through me. I lifted my hands tentatively and then began to remove my clothing. I undid my necktie, followed by my vest, shirt, and then breeches. All of the articles fell to the wooden floor, creating a pile to my right.

"Very good," Pan praised.

I hesitated before removing the last piece, now completely nude. I felt exposed, my muscles quivering with both fear and anticipation.

"Quaking like a virgin," Pan teased. "Bring the soap and towel, and come to the bed."

I obeyed him, grabbing both items and crossing the room to where he now waited for me. To *our* bed.

The one bed in the entire estate.

"Lay down," Pan said.

I took a deep breath, glaring as I climbed up onto the bed. My cock was already straining, and I felt my cheeks flush.

"Turn over," Pan said, chuckling. "Mmm. My little buck, your body is so lovely."

"Go to hell," I sneered as I rolled onto my back,

Pan went to the foot of the bed and grabbed me, pulling

me to the edge and then pushing my thighs back. I gasped, letting out a little whimper.

I was now completely and utterly exposed.

The Queen could rot in the very dark pits of hell for forcing me to endure such a matching. The Monster's Ball was her greatest hoax.

"Such a lovely hole for me to fill," Pan murmured. "But no. Not until you want me, little buck."

I would have bit out another curt remark, but he was already spreading the shaving soap over my ass and around my cock. I gasped, the coolness of it shocking me to my very core.

My cock began to pulse, aching.

"Pan," I whispered, swallowing hard.

"Yes?" he asked, grinning.

I glared, hating that grin. Hating the little fangs that were there and the way they glinted in the lantern light.

"You're a *monster*," I said, meaning for it to be an insult. Only, it came out as a pant.

"Yes, I am." He smiled and I felt the blade now, gasping as he started to shave me again.

I stayed still. So very still as he rid my body of any hairs. It was humiliating and terrible and...my cock was so incredibly hard, I could barely think straight.

I wanted him inside of me. I wanted to feel that monstrous shaft spread me wide, to be bred by the Satyr King.

Everything in my life had gone to hell, and this had to be the lowest of lows.... but I was having a harder time convincing myself of that in this moment.

He wiped the warm towel over my skin, cleaning the soap off and leaving me more bare than I had been in ages.

"Okay, little buck," Pan said. "That is all."

"Wait," I cried, propping myself up.

Pan paused, looking at me. "Yes?"

A witch. This Satyr had to be a witch. He had to have some sort of magic that made me crave his shaft.

Still...

"I want you," I said, now completely and utterly humiliated.

"Oh?" Pan chimed. His bright blue eyes slid down to my cock, a brow arching. "Beg me, little buck."

"Please," I said.

"No, no," he chuckled, taking a step back. "Beg me. Beg your King to breed your scoundrel hole. Beg for me to take mercy on a peasant like you, to bless you with the presence of my shaft."

"Absolutely not," I growled.

Pan smiled, shrugging. "So be it then. My cock knows my hand well."

I cursed under my breath as he headed towards the door.

"Wait," I snarled, sliding off the bed.

Pan paused and then turned towards me.

Was I, Ezra Fitzroy III, really going to fall on my knees to beg a Satyr King to take me?

Yes.

Gods damn it all to hell.

I slowly lowered myself to my knees, my caps hitting the floor with a thud.

"Please, Pan. Please breed my peasant hole. Please breed me until I'm worthy of being your Prince."

Pan was silent for a moment, victory blazing in his gaze. "Very well, little buck. How can I tell my fiancé no?"

Little Buck

P^{an}

My clothes fell to the floor in a heap. I stood completely exposed in front of my betrothed.

"For a scoundrel, you're so nervous," I teased, stepping closer.

He let out a soft grunt, parting his lips. His eyes feasted on my cock, his hand falling down to his own.

"I've never been with a monster," he whispered.

"You've never been with a King either. Your lucky day, hmm?"

"I want to taste you," he gasped. "Please let me."

His submission was beautiful. It was more satisfying than anything I had ever experienced. The look in his eyes, the way his chest rose and fell with breaths of need...

He was a gift, one that threatened to undo me.

"Open wide, peasant," I said.

He obeyed, his lips parting for me. The sight of him on his knees, hard and begging to taste my cock, was a sight enough to make me cum like a prepubescent faun. Instead, I held on tight to my restraint and leaned forward, filling his hot mouth with the head of my shaft.

"You take it so well," I groaned. "Your mouth was made for my cock, little buck."

Ezra groaned as he took me, my hips thrusting forward. His fingers dug into my thighs, the sounds he made driving me wild. I gripped his velvety hair, pumping into his mouth with a fervor before yanking free.

He drew in a sharp breath, panting. "Pan. *Please.* I need you to fill me."

"Get on the bed," I growled.

Ezra scrambled to his feet, his muscles flexing as he climbed onto the bed. I let out a happy groan, wanting to taste his perfect ass.

"On your hands and knees," I commanded.

He obeyed, positioning himself like so. I went to the edge of the bed, my eyes raking over every exposed inch of him. His cock throbbed between his thighs, his bare ass gleaming in the amber glow of our room.

I climbed onto our bed behind him but then paused, feeling a primal part of me rise up that had not in a long time.

"Oh dear," I breathed.

"What's wrong?"

"I might...my form might become more monstrous. I cannot control this."

"I don't care," he gasped. "Fuck me however you want."

His crude words had my cock throbbing and I let out a helpless moan, feeling my body start to grow. My muscles and bones snapped, and the horns on my head began to lengthen. I became larger, my fingers turning into talons.

I was the Satyr King, and this was my most monstrous form. The most primal part of me, reminiscent of a berserker, that I never let anyone see before, until now.

I let out a low growl, catching my reflection in the mirror across the room. Ezra let out a whimper beneath me, and I realized he was looking at the reflection too.

Mate.

He was my mate. *Mine.* This human harbored the very soul my own had been yearning for centuries.

"Are you scared?" I asked.

"No," he breathed. "Please take me."

I let out a painful grunt, dragging my claws down his back. His muscles shivered, his smooth skin disrupted by the angry red lines my talons left.

I leaned down, spreading his cheeks wide and ran my tongue between them. He let out a loud moan, pressing his head into the blankets. Still, he kept his ass propped up and his legs parted for me. *Such a good boy.*

I gripped his cock right as I drove my tongue inside of him. His back arched, his cry echoing through the room.

I wanted all of London to hear my scoundrel submit.

I wanted the entire ton to know that he was mine.

Never had I wanted someone so much in my entire life, and now? Now I would never be able to escape him. This desire clutched me in its infernal grip, driving me to the very edge of sanity. I wanted to consume him, to take him in every way possible.

He cried out again as I began to stroke his cock in the same rhythm that I thrust my tongue in and out. His body shivered, his breaths becoming ragged as he took what I gave.

I wanted to sit on the throne with him riding my cock.

I wanted him to suck my cock while wearing a crown.

I wanted him to *worship* me. To *love* me. No one else's love for me mattered now that I had Ezra.

My thoughts were going wild, desires pumping through me. Fantasies chasing reality, my dreams of finally having a mate coming true.

Mate.

The word pounded through my skull in the same way my heart pounded in my chest, strong and rhythmic.

Ezra was *mine*.

I pulled my tongue free and reached for the oil on the bedside table. I poured some onto his ass, lubing my cock. I moved closer, guiding the head of my cock to his hole.

"Please," he begged. He lifted his head, looking back at me.

"Are you certain?" I breathed.

"I have never been more so. *Take me.*"

I couldn't ask again. With a groan, I thrust forward and filled him with the first few inches of my cock. He cried out, finally abandoning his cares of being heard. His fingers dug into the blankets, his back muscles rippling with desire as he took me.

I held his hips, holding him in place as I thrust more of myself inside of him.

"It won't fit," he cried. "There's no way, my King."

"You will take it," I chuckled. "Your body was made for me, little buck. You will take it."

Ezra nodded, moaning again.

I moved slowly, giving him more of my cock. I could feel him pulsing around me, squeezing me tightly like a fist.

"You feel heavenly," I whispered, my head tipping back.

I could see our reflection, and was thankful I had mirrors placed over my bed.

He was truly being taken by a monster.

It had been centuries since I had seen myself like this. My horns curled back from my head, my haunches covered in dark fur. My talons, my fangs, my *cock*.

"Such a scandal," I said, grinning. "My scandalous little scoundrel begging for his hole to be filled."

"More," he whispered.

"More? I thought you said you could take no more."

"*More*," he growled, moving his ass back.

I let out a soft chuckle and dragged my hips back. I then drove forward, filling him until his ass was pressed against my body and he was impaled completely.

He was glorious. I sucked in a breath before repeating the motion, pulling my cock free before filling him again. The two of us found a rhythm, the sounds of our skin slapping against each other echoing around us. I grunted, digging my talons into him as I fucked him harder.

"I'm going to cum," he gasped. "*Pan*."

"Cum," I growled. "Cum everywhere, little buck."

He groaned helplessly, his muscles relaxing as I drove into him with force. He let out a curse as I reached down and gripped his cock, stroking him quickly.

With a sharp cry, he started to cum—his hot seed filling my hand and dripping down onto the blankets. I let out a satisfied hum, turned on even more by his release.

I growled, throwing my head back as I thrust into him once more. Carnal oblivion crashed into me as I buried myself to the hilt, my cum shooting out and filling his eager body.

The two of us collapsed in a heap, panting, and I felt my

body shifting back to its normal form. I slowly pulled out of Ezra, watching my cum drip from him.

He rolled to his side, breathing deeply. "Blazes...I've never...I've never been taken like that."

"I have never taken someone like that," I said, grinning as I sat back.

I looked down at his body, realizing that his cock was still hard.

As was mine.

He raised a brow, a daring gleam entering his eyes as he looked over me. He then moved closer, pushing me down onto the bed and straddling me.

I held up my hand, licking his cum. He watched in surprised awe, his eyes burning with lust.

"I am still angry with you," he murmured.

"Aw, and here I was thinking you'd let that go," I teased.

"No," he breathed, running his hands down my chest. "No, but I can't think right now of anything other than taking your cock again."

"Nothing is stopping you," I whispered.

His lips tugged into a smile and he leaned down, surprising me by swirling his tongue over one of my nipples. My own body surprised me, a cry leaving me as pleasure stabbed through me.

"Gods," I gasped as he continued.

He kissed across my chest, swirling his tongue over the other nipple. I cried out again, shocked by the burning pleasure. It was like he was igniting the flame, his tongue the spark.

"You like that," he rasped.

"More than you know," I growled.

He tugged my nipple between his teeth, and this time I arched, my cock now fully throbbing against him.

He reached between us, holding his cock against mine.

"I might just be a human," he whispered. "But I promise you, I do know some...things about pleasure."

"Well," I groaned. "I command you to show me everything you know. I have to ensure you truly know what you speak of."

His lips curved into a smile and he gave my nipple a bite before sucking, the sharp pain immediately smothered by a soothing pleasure.

He began to grind his hips, his cock rubbing against mine. He was hard and throbbing, his hand holding our shafts together.

"Good boy," I whispered, my words melting into a gasp as he continued to suck and grind. "Do you like pleasing me?"

"Yes," he mumbled between sucks.

His hand tightened around our cocks, his little humps becoming more desperate. Cream dripped from the tip of my cock, and I knew that it wouldn't be long before I was cumming all over him.

"You like being good for me," I rasped, watching him with carnal delight.

"Yes," he moaned.

"Even though you actually hate me for making you do all of these seemingly terrible things. Hate to be wed to the Satyr King."

"Forced into marriage," he growled. "Forced into one bed."

"Mmhmm. So much *force*."

I let out a helpless cry as he began to move his hips faster, our cocks rubbing against each other. He was starting to lose control, to lose the edge I'd let him believe he had.

He wanted to please me.

He wanted to be mine.

"Harder, little buck," I gasped. "Bite me as hard as you want. Do whatever you need to feel like you're in control of me, even though we both know the truth."

"Go to hell," he snarled, but his words barely had any ire to them.

He bit down on one of my nipples, his little teeth sending a flare of pain. I grinned for a moment— until I felt the first snaps of a mating bond taking root.

"Wait," I said with a startle. "Fiend seize it!"

I flipped him over, pinning him beneath me in one motion. Ezra gasped, his eyes widening.

I let out a dark growl, holding him beneath me. Our cocks throbbed against each other, our breaths ragged.

"Monsters create bonds with their mates through bites," I whispered. "I...felt something. We can continue but only if you want."

"I don't want...I don't want a mating bond," Ezra said, shaking his head.

The look of regret on his face was enough to almost kill me.

"It's a good thing," I whispered earnestly.

"No. I don't want to be mated to you."

"Well, you're doing a poor job of telling me so," I said.

He glared, letting out a frustrated breath. "Can you please just let us finish again?"

I narrowed my eyes.

I had wanted that mating bite, but this was one thing I wouldn't...*couldn't*...force him into doing.

I was manipulative, but I wasn't cruel.

I was desperate for him, but I needed him to want it.

"You're a bastard," I whispered, but I was already pushing his legs back again.

His cheeks flushed, his eyes burning with rage. The two of us glared at each other as I thrust my cock inside of him again, filling him without mercy. He cried out, his eyes fluttering closed for a moment as he took me.

"Go to hell," he whispered.

I grinned almost evilly now, gripping his cock. "I will meet you there, little buck."

He groaned as I savagely thrust into him, pumping in and out. I was already wild for him again, and this time I could feel my gentleness slipping.

His arms wound around my neck as I fucked him, holding on to the monster he swore he despised. I was his fiancé, his king, and would be the one he would give his heart to before he knew it.

Everything melted away as I filled him, losing myself to the passion between us. The two of us cried out together, and I gasped in wonder as I came again. His own cum shot out on a moan, coating our skin.

"I might be marrying you," he whispered when he had caught his breath. "I might be fucking you. But I will never love you."

He pushed me back and I pulled out of him, rolling to the side.

"Go to sleep," I said cheerfully, hiding just how deeply his words had stung. "Tomorrow, we promenade."

A Grand Entrance

E zra

"GOOD MORNING," PAN SAID CHEERFULLY AS I CAME INTO THE dining room.

He was already drinking a cup of coffee and eating breakfast, food stretching out over the table. I stood in the doorway for a moment, taking it all in.

My muscles were slightly sore from last night, and waking up alone had made me feel... something I could not describe.

I had also woken up hard.

I was reluctant to join Pan. After everything that had occurred in the last couple of days, last night had been the worst and best. The sex had been the best I'd ever had, and I could no longer deny having affections for the charmingly arrogant monster, but I still wished for my freedom.

Of course, if everything went well, then I would be more free—wouldn't I? That was the deal we had made.

And yet...

I let out a sigh and went to the chair on the opposite end of the table, plopping down into it.

"How did you sleep?" Pan asked, grinning. Always grinning.

I glared at him sleepily. "Pan, I am not awake enough currently to handle your endless jubilation. So, treat me as if I were a ghost."

He snorted, turning his gaze to one of his many servants who was now pouring a cup of coffee for me. I took it with a grumble of thanks, offering them a half smile before glaring back at Pan.

"Once you're more awake, we must discuss our plans for the day! We have our promenade at half past eleven, followed by a visit to the lavender fields. I love fresh lavender. Then, we will have some afternoon tea and—"

I could not take this right now.

I stood up and plucked a biscuit from the table and turned, taking my cup of coffee out of the room with me.

"Be ready in two hours!"

"I will," I barked, going down the hall.

I heard Pan's sigh as I left, but I ignored him.

I went outside to the back gardens, wandering until I found a bench by a fountain. I sat down, eating my biscuit while I stewed in my thoughts.

"You look rather miserable for someone who is engaged to a king."

I looked up, jarred by a voice I didn't recognize.

A man—no, a Satyr—was standing in one of the garden arches, watching me with a curious gaze. He reminded me of Pan, only he had darker hair, black fur instead of brown, and a scar that covered the left side of his face from eyebrow to the top of his upper lip.

Not to mention, he did not carry the cheery demeanor my fiancé had, he was more calculating and stoic.

"Not miserable," I lied.

Was it a lie? Was I actually miserable?

"Mind if I join you?" he asked, coming closer.

"Apologies, Sir. But who are you? I was looking for some time alone, and unless it is important, I would like to be left in silence." I didn't care if I were rude at this point, I was still waiting for the cup of coffee to make me less irritable.

"Someone that can help you escape the fate the Satyr King has forced upon you."

I narrowed my eyes. I wasn't a fool. A person did not say such a thing unless they had ill intentions.

I ate the rest of my biscuit, finished my cup of coffee, and stood. "I think I am perfectly capable of handling my fate. Good day."

I moved past him, but he grabbed my arm with a low growl. I turned, feeling rage work through me.

Yanking myself free, I let out a low growl. "How dare you."

"I am only here to help, Ezra Fitzroy," he snarled.

"I don't need your help. Touch me again and you will acquire a fate worse than mine. Now. *Good day.*"

I left him standing there, heading back to the house. Now, I was in an even worse mood, and feeling slightly concerned that there was a random rake on our estate.

Our estate.

A hiss parted my lips as I went back through the double doors, running straight into Pan.

His hands clamped my arms, steadying me. "Oh hello, my little buck. You seem flustered. Are you okay?"

I scoffed, pulling myself free, and moved past him. "No, just tired of Satyrs' grabbing me. I shall be ready soon."

I stewed with my thoughts as I rushed upstairs and found my clothing already laid out on our bed.

Pan's bed. Not our bed.

Within the hour, I was bathed and dressed. I paused at the mirror, gazing at my jaw. I was still smooth from where Pan had shaved me last night.

My cock throbbed just thinking about it.

Gods damn it all to hell. The monster had ruined me.

"Are you certain you're okay?"

I turned to see Pan leaning against the doorway, his gaze roaming over me. I felt a wave of heat, of *need*.

"I am," I said.

"Are you sore? Our activities were rather....rough last night."

"I am... somewhat. But in a good way. No, I am merely annoyed with everyone and everything. And I hate walks in the garden. Promenades are boring."

"They are when you don't know how to enjoy them," Pan chuckled. "I promise that you will not be bored this time. And besides, don't you wish to see your father getting vexed yet again? I'm sure our carriage will appeal more to the ton than his."

I snorted. I had never considered myself to be a petty soul, but hearing Pan say such words brought a joy that had me considering a change of heart. I *did* like seeing my father bristle at Pan's lackadaisical commands.

"Perhaps," I said, fighting a smile.

Pan came closer, crossing the room until he stood behind me. Our gazes met in the mirror, and my cheeks flushed red as thoughts of last night flooded my mind.

He cocked his head, his eyes softening. "Oh little buck. We can't right now."

"I don't want to," I lied.

"Of course," he whispered.

I watched as he raised his hand, warmth settling on my hip.

It comforted me, even though the layers of my clothing.

"You look regal," he murmured.

I let out a breath and leaned forward, gripping the sides of the sink. He moved closer, his body pressing against mine.

"You do very bad things to me," he said.

I could feel his cock through his breeches, fitting snugly against me.

I ached to be filled by him again.

"I promise to breed you when we return," he said.

I wanted to tell him to go to hell. I wanted to fight him. To turn and shove him away, and leave for good.

But I couldn't move a muscle.

Not when he touched me like this.

Not when his cock felt so good against my ass.

"We must go," I whispered.

"Yes," Pan sighed. "Come."

"I *can't*."

"No," he chuckled. "Come *with* me because we have to leave."

I didn't have a chance to respond, as he was already grabbing my hand and leading me from the room.

We went downstairs and to the carriage awaiting to take us to the park. This one had an open top, one that would allow all of the ton to see us.

It was like a theater show. A play for the rich and wealthy to show off their golden lives from inside their high walled gardens. Our carriage would deliver us and then we would walk around pretending to be perfectly happy. I despised it, but...

Pan helped me into the carriage, winking at me as he climbed in next to me.

Pan was King, which meant he could get away with far more than many of us. Perhaps this *would* be more fun than before.

A minotaur closed the carriage door, giving Pan a look I couldn't read.

"Oh," Pan said. "Bernard. After we promenade, I am taking Ezra to the lavender fields. I haven't been in quite some time, and we will require a change of clothing and another carriage."

"I will have them ready, Your Majesty."

"Thank you."

"And lunch as well?"

"Ah. Yes. Perhaps a basket of goods for us. Our reward for suffering the ton will be a picnic."

Bernard nodded, his horns glinting in the morning light. "Yes, Your Majesty."

Pan winked at him and then turned to address our driver. "Take it slow, good sir. We must be the last ones to arrive so as to make a grand entrance."

"Yes, Your Majesty."

Our carriage started down the street, the sounds of horses' hooves on stone a familiar and somewhat comforting noise. I relaxed in my seat, but Pan leaned forward, drawing out a parasol from gods knew where.

"Here you are," he said, popping it open. "Can't have you burning in the sun."

"I assure you I am fine."

"Your red cheeks say otherwise."

"Pan," I chuckled. "I merely tan in the sun. I am not a fair skinned maiden."

"It doesn't hurt anything," he teased, forcing me to take it.

I sighed, holding it despite not wanting to. Pan smirked in victory and leaned forward.

"I'd like to steal a kiss."

"In front of gods and everyone?" I asked, looking around us. "You're mad. We are in Westminster, Pan. Everyone will watch us. Are you trying to get us on the front page of the High Tea again?"

"Yes," he said.

I sighed, but leaned towards his mouth regardless. Our lips brushed over each other, and despite all of the anger and frustration of the morning, I found myself melting into the feel and taste of him. Into the touch of his lips, the way his mouth fit against mine.

He deepened our kiss, drawing a groan from me.

My cock throbbed.

I pulled back immediately with a gasp, my head spinning.

Pan smirked and leaned back, knowing he had won. What he had won, I wasn't sure.

Perhaps my submission.

I glared at him, forcing my gaze to look at the world around us. It was already warm, the air sticky. Summer mornings were best spent in the country, in my opinion, but with all of the events the Monsters Ball had stirred, I was sure that it would be some time before I made it out of London.

What would the land of Essex be like?

"What is your kingdom like?" I asked.

Pan raised a brow. "Huh. I didn't think you would care."

71

"I do care," I grumbled.

"Well. There are cities, like London. But they aren't polluted. I don't allow the air to be besieged by smog, or for the streets to be run with shite. Those that live in the country are doing well for themselves, just as those in the city. Most monsters are more open to sexual relations, and it is not uncommon to see throuples or more raising children together. It is...quite different from the world you live in."

Everything that he spoke of sounded...nice. Like a utopia.

"I think that you would find that you are no longer regarded as a scoundrel there. Even with the drinking."

"I don't actually drink that much," I muttered. "It's more that I enjoy frequenting the clubs in order to vex my father. And well... Seeing my cousin best men in gambling has always provided me much joy."

"Ah yes. Ambrose's bride. I do wonder how that will go. My friend can be...well... the Lord lives in his own mind much of the time."

"Phoebe will be fine," I said. "She can handle anyone, monster or man."

"You are quite fond of her."

"I am," I said, nodding. "Her and her brothers are like my own siblings. My step brother and sister are much younger than me. My cousins were who I relied on when my mother passed. They helped me."

"I'm glad that you have good family members," Pan said, staring off into the distance. "Even if some of them are asinine."

I frowned, unsure of what to make of his expression. "Do you not have a good family?"

"My brother hates me," he said simply. "And I have no

other kin. My mother passed some time ago as did my father, passing his crown to me. It has been ages."

"That must be difficult."

"Only in that my brother wishes to see me perish."

"What did you ever do to him?" I asked, curious.

"Oh," Pan chuckled, shrugging. "I am not sure, to be honest. We got along just fine as younglings, pranking each other. But then we grew up. He went away, I took my place as King. And well...it wasn't until recently that he challenged me for the crown."

I thought back to the satyr in the garden. Was that his brother?

If so, I did not like him.

"I think I might have met—"

"We are here, Your Majesty," the carriage driver interrupted.

I let out a breath as Pan turned, that somewhat evil grin returning. "AH! We are!" He laughed, clapping his hands as the carriage slowed to a halt. "Well, little buck. Let's give the ton something to talk about, shall we?"

Promenade

P^{an}

IT WAS A TRULY LOVELY SUMMER MORNING DESPITE THE HEAT. I gazed out over the gardens, watching as ladies in exuberant dresses and coiffed hair walked with their lords, their mamas ever watchful. Ezra and I had already turned many heads, and I loved the thrill I got from watching the gossip mongers a titter.

Still, my plan was working.

Slowly, but surely, Ezra's reputation as a scoundrel was turning into something worthy of his stature. The Crown Prince—someone they would all have to bow to.

I gasped, seeing the very tent I had planned on visiting.

"Lottie is here," I said, with obvious excitement. "Come on."

Ezra grumbled as I hurried my steps, dragging him along with me.

The two of us made our way to the Queen's tent, and I grinned as I approached.

Her gaze fell on me, and I watched as her pinched expression softened . "Pan," she said. "My monster King. And his betrothed! SOMEONE GET MY GUESTS CHAIRS."

I ignored the fluttering of her servants as they all immediately jumped to obey, placing two chairs near Lottie for Ezra and I to sit. I went to her, kneeling down. "My human Queen."

"Oh good goddess," she laughed, but she offered me her hand.

I gave her a kiss, wiggled my brow, and then turned to look at Ezra.

He was sweating, his posture both stiff and nervous. He bowed, mumbling my queen.

"He's so nervous," she teased.

"And who wouldn't be, Lottie?" I said, taking my seat. Ezra stood awkwardly for a moment, but I motioned to the chair next to me. "Come on, Lord Fitzroy, please sit."

Ezra nodded and took the chair, fumbling with his parasol. Lottie raised a perfectly drawn brow.

"So tell me," she said. "How does one of my favorite royal friends end up with the scoundrel of the ton."

"Fate," I said, grinning. I reached over, taking Ezra's hand in mine. He immediately squeezed it, so I caressed the back of his hand with my thumb, hoping he would relax. "It was meant to be. The Ball worked in my favor."

"Good. There have been many this season who were left unwed! This season might have been boring if it weren't for the Monster's Ball."

Ezra was now squeezing the life out of my hand. I looked over at him, trying to urge him to be calm.

I wished we had our mated bond, so he would be able to take comfort in me.

"Can we get my fiancé a beverage, please?" I asked.

One of the ladies in waiting immediately sprang up, bringing Ezra a flute of cider. He took it, murmuring his thanks.

"I can't complain," I said. "Although, I'm afraid the two of us are the source of many new rumors."

"I would hope so," she laughed. "The High Tea has been much more interesting as of late. To think they all believe Ezra ruined you..."

"Ha! Well, you know the truth without even having to ask," I chuckled.

Ezra let out a breath, and I was happy to see him smirk.

"Poor man," she said, giving him a once over. "And how is he in bed, Lord Fitzroy?"

Ezra choked on his drink, coughing. I thumped his back in concern.

"Good heavens, my love," I said. "*Swallow*."

I waited for him to collect himself, and to my delight, he obeyed.

"Gods," Ezra breathed. "My apologies, Your Majesty. I was caught off guard."

Lottie smirked, shrugging. "I am merely curious. You see, I have seen Pan seduce so many in my time as his friend. You must know I'm sure that will continue, but with your own reputation, I am sure you don't mind."

I felt my anger flare, and I stilled.

Ezra surprised me by leaning forward, his tone unyielding. "No. We will be true to one another. Neither one of us will be stepping out on the other. He is *mine*."

His words shocked me.

"Is this true, Pan?"

I looked at him, his words burning through me. Ezra looked up at me, his anger palpable.

He was jealous at the thought of me being with another.

"Yes. It is true," I whispered. "He is mine, Lottie. From now until the end of time."

She cocked her head, sighing. "Interesting. A love match, then. Fate truly is strange, wouldn't you agree? The Satyr King no longer the grand seducer."

"No," I said. "I am his as much as he is mine."

Silence settled over us. I held her piercing gaze, allowing her to see my conviction.

"Very well," she said, relaxing. "You both have my blessing. Not that you need it, Pan. But it will be good for you. Perhaps the vipers surrounding us will spread their venom elsewhere."

"Thank you, Lottie," I said, rising from my seat. "If you don't mind, I believe we must continue our walk through the gardens."

She gave us a slight nod as I took Ezra's hand, leading him from the tent.

Silence settled over us as we started on the path again. We passed couples, mamas, families— all of which gave us their nods and curtsies.

"I thought you said this would be fun," Ezra mumbled.

"I thought you hated me," I responded.

He was silent again as we went past another couple.

"I do hate you," he finally said.

"Your words to the Queen didn't sound like hate."

"I was just lying of course," he muttered.

"Of course," I said with a grin. "I would expect nothing less of you."

He bristled at that, but didn't have time to argue as his

father and stepmother appeared along the path, followed by his two step siblings.

"AH! Our dear family," I exclaimed.

"Good morning, Your Majesty," Helen said, offering us a bow. "And stepson."

"Good morning," Ezra said. He stood up a little straighter, his arm looping tighter in mine. "Father. We have just received our blessings from Her Majesty the Queen."

John Fitzroy paled, his eyes narrowing on his eldest son. "Really? You don't jest."

"Of course he doesn't," I said. "Ezra isn't a liar. The Queen is most excited for our union and believes it will be good for our kingdoms. You should be proud to have a Prince for a son."

"I am proud, of course," he said, despite the way his brows drew together and the pinching of his mouth.

"Good. And good morning, little lord and lady!"

Elizabeth and little John grinned up at me, giving me a curtsey and a bow.

"Uncle James, Phoebe, and William will be joining us soon," Helen said, offering me a somewhat kind smile. "Would you be so inclined to stroll together?"

"That sounds wonderful," I said. "But I'm afraid we must decline. Ezra and I have much needed business to attend to, and we were simply coming here to make an appearance before the Queen."

Ezra's father scoffed, but Ezra chuckled.

"Right. Sorry father, my duties as a Prince are calling. Elizabeth, John—I will see you both Sunday at the wedding."

I watched happily as they both gave their older brother hugs and then went about rambling. I winked at his father and stepmother, and then pulled him along, steering him back to where our carriage waited.

"Okay," Ezra chuckled. "That was fun. His expression was one of absolute torture."

"Well, I did invite them to promenade only to then promptly leave," I said. "But...well, it is true. The lavender fields await us, along with our lunch."

"Indeed," Ezra said happily.

I stole a glance at him, enjoying how relaxed he appeared at the moment.

I could imagine us like this, happy and carefree, always. Someone to share my joys with, to give my love to. Sunday, we would be wed, but I hoped that he would offer his heart to me as well, not just his hand.

I was falling for him. Seven hells, I had already fallen for him. The moment I saw him at the Ball, I knew.

And the longer I knew him... The more I wanted his love.

Lavendar

E zra

It was a short ride to the lavender fields that Pan was determined to take me too, but I found I had enjoyed the time with him today. And much to my dismay, the two of us had fallen into conversations easily.

I kept reminding myself that he was a monster. That I was being forced to marry him. That he had manipulated me and others, even going so far as to ensure there was only one bed for us to sleep in. Still...

I yearned for him. I wanted to feel his skin against mine, to see his body turn back into the beastly form he had last night. I had watched him in the mirror as he had taken me, as he had succumbed to his most primal parts.

And I had loved every moment of it.

The intimate moments haunted me now.

The scent of lavender picked up on the summer breeze

and I breathed it in, letting out a satisfied hum as our carriage stopped. We got out and Pan grabbed the basket that Bernard had prepared for us.

"We still need to change," I said.

"We will," Pan said, giving a nod to the driver.

The carriage started again, leaving the two of us on the road that divided the fields. There wasn't another soul in sight, and it felt as if it were just the two of us in this world.

"Are we really going to just walk through the fields?" I asked. "Isn't that very un-kingly?"

"I don't care," Pan snorted. "Come on, little buck."

"I'd dare say you're courting me," I muttered as I followed him.

The two of us made our way through the field, Pan leading us towards a massive tree that sat in the center. He carried our basket of food and clothes without a care in the world, his posture relaxed.

As if my body was in harmony with his, I found myself finally relaxing as well.

We made it to the tree and he sat the basket down, pulling out a blanket.

"You are truly something else," I said, shaking my head in amusement at his diligence.

"Sit," he said.

I sat down next to him, spreading my legs out. I let out a happy sigh, looking up at the tree that stretched above us.

"Let's see what Bernard packed for us," Pan said, pulling out plates and food.

I smiled as I watched him and then looked out at the fields surrounding us. The purple and pink against the idyllic blue skies was enough to make me forget about all of the problems from the last couple of days, and to calm the lingering jealousy from the Queen's remarks.

Pan had been shocked by what I had said, but I had been even more so. The idea of him even looking at another in such a way had stirred up fury in me.

He moved closer to me, sitting across so that our legs touched. I looked down at his hooves, at the soft fur that covered him.

"I like it when you look at me like that," he said as he spread various cheeses out on a plate. He then pulled out fresh baked bread and a knife, cutting slices for us.

"Look at you how?" I asked.

"As if you want me."

I did want him.

That thought startled me, but I didn't fight it this time. I had been fighting everything for so long, and enjoying this....would it truly hurt me?

I took a piece of bread with a slice of cheese, biting into it, and let out a moan. The flavors were wonderful and Bernard truly had a refined palette.

"Bernard is good at choosing even simple things," Pan said.

"That he is."

"He's been with me for a long time. A most trusted butler. His daughter will be joining the ton next season."

"Is that allowed?" I asked, surprised.

"Yes," Pan said. "His official title is that he is an advisor to the King, to fit in with how the Queen runs her world. He serves me and looks out for me, so he is most trusted. And his daughter is a fine lady."

"Do you treat all your servants like you care?"

"Of course," Pan answered, scowling. "They are all just making their wages to support their families. Here, try this jam."

Pan spread apricot jam out on a pastry, holding it to my mouth. I bit into it, our eyes locking as I tasted it.

It was exquisite.

Our eyes never left each other as he held the butter knife up, licking the jam from it.

I felt my cock throb as I swallowed.

"It's wonderful," I whispered.

Pan leaned closer, our lips a breath apart. My breath hitched, my heart pounding in my chest.

"I'm not a liar," I whispered.

"I know that."

"I don't hate you."

"I know that as well, little buck."

"*I want you.*"

Saying that lifted a weight from my shoulders.

Pan let out a soft grunt. "Say it again."

"I want you, Pan."

He swallowed hard. Part of me waited to see if he would smile, to see if he would give me that victorious look...but his expression remained vulnerable.

"I want you," I said again. "I want you. I might not later. But in this very moment, I want you."

He closed the gap between us, our lips crashing together. I groaned as I gave in to him, letting myself truly be with him, mind and body one. I let go of the anger, the guilt of disappointing my father, the feeling of being lost. I let it all go, simply sinking into the arms of my monster.

Pan pushed me back onto the blanket, pinning me beneath him. The two of us moaned, our kiss becoming desperate. I felt his cock swelling against mine, and I ground my hips against him.

"Gods," Pan breathed.

He sat up for a moment, yanking off his waist coat. I
pulled mine off as well, undoing the cravat around my neck.

"Strip," he growled. "No one will see us, the fields are
currently off limits but for us."

"You took the whole fields for us?!"

"Yes," Pan breathed. "Undress, little buck. Now."

We both stripped hurriedly, tossing our clothes to the
side. The moment the last of the fabric came off, Pan pulled
me back down onto the blanket, rolling me beneath him.

I reached between us, gripping his cock. A soft growl
emanated from his chest as he kissed me, our mouths
hungry. His teeth tugged on my bottom lip, and I whimpered at the little bite of pain.

It felt *good*.

Pan arrested my wrists, pushing them over my head and
holding them there. We stared at each other for a moment,
searching for any hesitance. Searching for something that
said we shouldn't continue, but there was nothing there.

"You like pain," he whispered.

"A little," I breathed.

His bright blue eyes gleamed with excitement. "Now, I
wish we were at my home in Essex. I have...items I must
show you. But, we will make do until then."

The mention of Essex and a life beyond this Sunday
made my heart beat a little faster. I felt the uneasiness
return, but it went up in smoke as Pan's hand wrapped
around my cock.

I arched beneath him, my arms still pinned by his other
hand.

"Good boy," he murmured.

My breath hitched on a groan, my hips thrusting up
again as he started to stroke me. His cock was hard against
me, and I was desperate to taste him again, but having him

THE SCOUNDREL AND THE SATYR KING

touch me like this... *control* me like this... I wanted everything he had to give.

"You're beautiful," Pan breathed.

I should have bristled at his words, but instead tears blurred my vision. Pan made a soft tsk and stole a kiss again, his hand still stroking me up and down. He was slow and steady, the rhythm building towards a crescendo I longed for.

A tear slipped down my cheek, but he kissed it away. He pressed his forehead to mine, our breaths mingling as he continued to stroke.

"My beautiful little buck," he said gently. "You just want someone that will care for you. That will accept you."

"Stop," I whimpered, more tears streaming.

His hand paused, but that only frustrated me.

"No," I breathed. "No, no. Don't stop touching me. I just...my heart feels like it might burst from my chest when you say such things."

"Has no one ever spoken to you in this way?" Pan asked.

No. No one had ever dared.

"Has no one ever told you that you deserve happiness? That you should be cherished, like the moon cherishes her stars?"

Pan released my hands and cupped my face, forcing me to look at him.

"Do you know how much you mean to me already, Ezra? I've been waiting for you all my life, to finally feel a tangible connection with a soul that is all mine. I have been searching, and even with all the lustful passions I have shared over the years, all of them pale in comparison to even simply being gazed upon by you. I ache for your acceptance, to hear you say that you want me how I want you. My entire being was created to be with yours, to create a life of love with you."

"*Pan*," I whispered.

"I want you, Ezra Fitzroy. I desire you in ways I did not believe possible. I know that the Monsters Ball was not what you wanted. I know that the idea of marriage and 'settling' does not appeal to you. But I do so solemnly swear that I will make you happy. I give you my word I will do everything in my power to make you smile."

"You do make me smile, you fool-headed satyr," I said, my lips tugging into one now. "I simply don't know what to do with you. You frustrate me, make me feel as if I'm going to explode. But, the longer I know you, the more I find that I adore you. No, this is not what I wanted at first, but I am not against you now. How can I be?"

Pan swallowed hard, giving a small nod.

I reached up, running my fingertips over his face. I pressed my palm against his jaw and he closed his eyes, breathing in my scent.

"Mate me," I said. "I know you wanted to last night. You spoke of a bond."

"A mating bond," Pan said, his eyes flying open. "Ezra, you do not understand what you ask for. It will bring us even closer in ways that are difficult to describe to a human."

"I want it," I said.

"Last night, you spoke of it as if it were damning."

"I was angry last night," I said. "I'm not so angry now. I'm...starting to accept this."

Pan shook his head, even though he looked tortured by it. "I will mate you if you ever fall in love with me, but I would despise myself for tying your soul to mine without that. Perhaps in the future, my love. But not now."

Love. I had never believed I might experience the feeling of it. I had always found couples that said they loved each other to be annoying, and had even believed they were liars.

My mother had said she loved my father.

He had been different then. Still harsh. Still an ass. But... she had softened him.

Was that what love was? Sharing a life with someone that made you a better person?

"Let me please you," Pan said. "And forget of the mating bond. We only have a couple of days before we marry, and I would like to make it as smooth as possible. If nothing more than to avoid the ton."

"And here I was thinking you liked for them to talk about you," I teased.

"I do. But, I have found that I don't like them talking about you. Had the Queen been anyone else... I cannot say my temper would have been controlled."

That was true for me as well. Her words had enraged me.

"I cannot share," Pan said simply. "I will not share. I might enjoy watching others, if you permit it and are by my side. But you are mine."

"I am," I said.

Saying it made it feel real.

"But," I said, sliding my hands down between us and gripping his cock. "You are mine, my Satyr King. I have never felt jealousy until now."

Pan's lips tugged into a knowing smile. "You know we are not objects that can possess each other."

I gave him a light shove, rolling him over so that I was now seated on top, straddling him.

"I do know that," I said, stroking his cock behind me. It

throbbed against my palm, his skin flushing as he began to become more needy. "We are not land to be owned."

"No," Pan whispered, watching me with a sense of wonder. "Are you going to ride my cock, little buck?"

"Yes," I chuckled.

"Then let me get you ready for my cock first."

Riding his King

Pan

EZRA GASPED AS I THRUST MY TONGUE INSIDE OF HIM, FORCING him to hover over my face as he stroked my cock. His muscles trembled, his cry echoing through the lavender fields.

This had been the grandest idea I had had so far, and hearing him be honest overwhelmed me with joy.

These were glimpses of the life we could have, the life that I craved. With *him*.

Ezra let out a crude curse, his gasps making me smile as I teased him. My fingers dug into his hips, holding him in place as I continued to play with him.

"Pan," he cried. "*Please.*"

He begged for my cock so well. And now, knowing that perhaps he liked a little pain...

I had to get us through Sunday and to my home where

all of my equipment was kept. I'd had a throne fashioned to bind the one sitting on it in place, making them vulnerable to whomever they were with. I had ropes, leather paddles, and items that suddenly gained a new vibrant life in my mind.

I would never grow bored of being with Ezra, and I wanted to find out everything that made his cock hard.

I lifted him with ease, turning his body so that he was straddling me again. I gripped my cock and pressed the head against him.

His head fell back, his pleasure making me smile.

He was losing himself to us—to the passion, to the heat that would surely consume us in its carnal intensity. His tan skin was dappled with shadows from the tree that covered us, his hair mussed from our rolling over each other.

"Please," he gasped. "I need every inch, Pan."

He slowly began to ease down on my cock, biting his lower lip with a suppressed moan as he took me.

"Good boy," I breathed. "My Prince. You do so well taking your King's cock."

He cried out as half of my cock buried inside of him. I let out a sharp groan, trying my best to control my urge to thrust up and fill him completely. I wanted to fill him with my seed, to breed him over and over.

"Good," I rasped. "Look at me, Ezra."

He obeyed immediately, our gazes locking. I held his hips as he took more, his body sinking down until finally, he was completely sheathed.

"You're so tight," I whispered. "You feel so good."

He whimpered, his cheeks flushed from the heat of the day and from our sensual fervor.

"Ride me," I whispered. "Ride your King. Take whatever rhythm you want, little buck. My cock is yours."

He nodded and leaned back, planting his hands on my thighs. He began to move up and down, impaling himself on my cock slowly.

I groaned, watching as his hard cock bounced with his movements. Pleasure worked through me, my blood burning with our lovemaking. The affliction of our passion, like nothing before, leaving me wanting more.

He began to move faster and harder, taking my monstrous cock repeatedly with soft moans and cries.

"Be louder," I rasped. "The whole world is deaf to our cries. Scream if you want."

He let out a sharper cry, my words freeing him. He grunted as he rode me, the sounds of our mating making me even harder.

He was glorious. I groaned as heat flared through me again, Ezra driving me to the edge of cumming. I was so close, right there—but I needed more.

I grabbed his hips and thrust up. Ezra gasped and leaned forward, his hands pressing against my chest as I took control. His expression was one of desirous oblivion, our moans and cries blending together as I began to fuck him harder.

"Breed me," he cried. "Please! I need you to fill me!"

His words sent me into an almost beastial frenzy, the need to take him becoming the very center of my being. I gasped as I thrust into him, feeling myself getting closer and closer.

"I'm going to cum," I moaned. "I'm going to fill you, little buck."

"*Please.*"

I fell into a brutal rhythm until finally— I let out a sharp cry as I started to cum. I held Ezra still as I filled him, groaning as he took my hot cum.

"Cum," I commanded.

He reached down and gripped his cock, jerking it quickly until he started to cum. I watched as he came over my stomach and chest, so much of it covering me.

"Good boy," I rasped, still panting.

The two of us relaxed and I pulled him free, watching as my cum dripped from him. He rolled to the side, the two of us lying next to each other, trying to catch our breaths.

My head was spinning. I felt like I was floating on the clouds, my entire body buzzing with life.

Ezra suddenly let out a laugh, one that had me looking over at him.

He grinned, and I realized this was the first time I'd seen him look truly happy and carefree.

My eyes softened and I smiled. He chuckled again and then looked over at me, his hand sliding into mine.

"This is quite preposterous you know," he teased. "For you to be wedlocked to me so soon. For us to be doing these activities out of marriage. Such a scandal."

"We are," I said. "Such a scandal."

He laughed again, squeezing my hand. "It's not so bad."

"No," I said, smirking. "No, it's not."

"What if we were found like this?"

"Oh, I would simply say that a bee was on you and we had to strip to rid you of the little bugger!"

"And how would you explain our seed everywhere?"

"We spilled the pastry icing my loyal butler packed for our picnic."

"Ah, I see," he snorted. "Clever, you are."

"I have my moments."

The two of us chuckled again and then fell into a comfortable silence, one that was only interrupted by the occasional breeze that ruffled the branches above us.

"I think I am falling for you, even though I have tried not to."

I looked over at him again, studying him. "Love isn't a poison, Ezra. It's a gift."

Ezra sighed, squeezing my hand again. "I didn't believe the notion to be true until today."

"It is quite real, I assure you. I have seen plenty of monsters find their fated mates, their true loves. It is beautiful."

"I haven't seen it very often."

"That's because your society prizes status over heart. It does not matter if there is love, so long as the children can carry on a grand name. And yes, some monsters do the same. But many wait until they find someone they share a bond with. And well, some wait centuries."

"Centuries?!" Ezra scoffed. "That is unfathomable to me. You creatures live for so long."

"We do," I said. "Bonded humans do as well. They share in the lifespans of their monstrous mates. There are some humans that were mated to monsters that have been around almost as long as me."

"Like who?" Ezra asked.

"Oh, hmm. There is one Lady Bellevue, I believe her name to be. She is married to a Viscount, and well—those two have been around for a very long time."

"Interesting," Ezra said, shaking his head. "How did she know of monsters? Our societies were apart for so long."

"Their story is one of a poor girl being whisked off by a monster, and it actually ending in a happily ever after. Not all monsters are good or kind. Some are, by nature, very *monstrous,* with nothing but desire to harm everyone around them."

I thought of my brother and his hatred for me. His

hatred for my kingdom and the monster and human matches that sometimes occurred.

He believed monsters should only love monsters, and humans should only love humans.

"I'm glad you are a good one," Ezra said. "I suppose I am lucky."

I turned onto my side, propping my torso up so that I could look down at him. He fit snugly against me, his expression still relaxed.

"Are you?" I asked.

"I am," he said. "I know...I have been difficult. But perhaps I am having a change of heart."

"We have all the time in the world," I said. "We will make ourselves happy, Ezra. I will do what I can for you."

He nodded, turning so that he could curl into me.

"Let us nap," I said gently. "Nap, and then we will make our way home. Tomorrow will be a big day, our last days unmarried."

Ezra only nodded, already growing sleepy. I was hesitant for a moment, but then I pulled him close, holding him to me as he fell asleep.

Monsters and Men

E zra

Tomorrow, I would be wed to the Satyr King— but I was no longer angry about it.

Yesterday, I had spent most of my time with Pan and found that I was not miserable. In fact, I had been happy and, for the first time, counting on fate's conception of my future.

Something had changed within me. I wasn't sure if it were me accepting my situation, or that I actually wanted it.

We would have a small gathering before the Archbishop in the morning, and then we would begin our journey to Essex. It would be a few days' ride, including stops at inns along the way.

I let out a soft sigh and sat up in bed, looking around at our room.

Our room.

This time I didn't chastise myself for thinking such things.

Pan had left our bed earlier, going to take care of some items that he'd called 'dull King things'. It was the first time I'd seen him even slightly disgruntled, but he had claimed it was because he didn't want to leave my side.

I hadn't wanted him to either. I was beginning to crave his company, and waking up alone made my chest ache.

"Good morning, my Lord."

I looked up, not surprised to see a creature with horns, wings, and pale green skin waiting. He was wearing a nice waistcoat and clothing, and came into the room to open the curtains.

"I have coffee and breakfast waiting for you, my Lord. Our Majesty has asked me to inform you that he will be back much later than he originally believed, but to please make yourself at home."

"Has something happened?" I asked, feeling a flare of concern.

He hesitated, but relented. "The King's brother has come to London without seeking our Majesty out. It is offensive. The King's brother has also asked for an audience with Her Majesty Queen Charlotte."

"Strange," I said, scowling.

I thought back to the satyr in the gardens yesterday morning.

"You have no worries, my Lord. I am confident our King will take care of any troubles."

"Yes, I'm sure," I mumbled, still frowning.

"Should you like your breakfast, my Lord?"

"Yes. And then, I would like to bathe, please. Thank you for your help."

"Of course, my Lord."

"What's your name?"

"Moss, my Lord. I am a woodland fae from Essex."

I nodded, offering him a smile. "Do you like working for the King?"

"He is kind," Moss said. "He has helped my family. And all who serve him are treated the same way."

I already knew that to be true, but I liked hearing it first-hand.

Pan was a kind king, even though he liked to vex others.

Well, perhaps he liked vexing humans specifically.

"Thank you," I said.

I spent the next hour eating breakfast in bed and then taking a hot bath in one of the copper tubs. Pan obviously loved the scent of lavender, as most of his soaps were scented with it. I found one bar that smelled of honey, and used it instead.

Now, I was dressed, and growing impatient.

Concerned, really.

Pan had mentioned his brother several times now, and it seemed as though the monster was a problem.

I roamed the house until I found myself in a library. I hummed to myself, raising my brows as I looked around.

This was magnificent. It was a small library, but the shelves were packed with volumes of literary works—much of which appeared to be from creatures.

I went to one of the shelves, running my fingertips over the spine.

"Anything of interest to you?"

I turned, the voice sending a wave of anger through me.

The satyr from the gardens was here, standing in the doorway.

I glared at him. "What are you doing in my home?"

He raised a dark brow, regarding me with open malice, which he had obviously hidden yesterday.

"This isn't your home, human," he said, stepping inside and closing the doors behind him.

I felt a trickle of fear. I had fought many brawls and had won most of them, but never against a monster. If he was as strong as Pan, then this would not go well.

"Is there something that you need?" I asked. "I am betrothed to the King, and this is inappropriate."

He barked out a laugh, stepping closer to me. His hands were behind his back, his hooves clicking on the marble floors.

"I doubt that you, of all people, care about what is inappropriate. I have seen what you have been doing with my brother."

My muscles tensed and I faced him despite the way my heart began to beat faster.

This bastard was in fact Pan's brother.

"I heard that Pan was looking for you," I said nonchalantly, acting as if his presence did not bother me at all.

"Oh, I'm sure," he said. "I mean. He did invite me to the dinner the other night, but I had...other business to attend to. Such as hiring someone to help me murder you. And of course, it wasn't easy to find some bloke that despised you. A scorned brother, just like me, in fact."

I began to slowly move across the library, looking for some sort of weapon without making it obvious I was doing so.

"I am confused as to why you wish me harm," I said. "I have never done anything to you. I don't even know your name."

"My name is Ben. And you make my brother happy, and that simply cannot stand. You see, everything Pan has ever wanted, he gets. And that stops now. It's my turn to take the throne, and if he doesn't have his mate, he will not be able to stop me."

I took a step back from him, scowling. "What do you mean? If he doesn't have his mate?"

Ben regarded me for a moment, and then barked out a laugh. "Oh gods. Did Pan not tell you?"

"Tell me *what*?" I snarled.

"The whole reason for the absurdness. If he doesn't mate with someone soon, I will take the crown from him. There is a law—that if the ruler is unmated for 500 years, then they can be challenged by other blood."

I was torn between being shocked by the revelation and being surprised by Pan's age.

"That is a ridiculous law," I said.

Ben shrugged, grinning as he stepped closer.

"I think I like it."

"What did Pan ever do to you?" I asked. "He is kind and loving, and he has helped many."

"He cast me out of the kingdom!" Ben roared, closing the gap between us. He slammed me against one of the shelves, and I stilled as I felt a cold blade against my neck. "He banned me for years. All because I don't believe humans are good enough for us. I'm doing him a favor. You aren't worthy of a King, you pathetic scoundrel. Do you know how much I have heard about you? About what they say?"

I let out an angry hiss, shoving against him. It was no use though, he was stronger, and now had me pinned completely.

He leaned in closer, his breath hot against my ear. "They say that you're worthless. That you've thrown away the wealth your father has earned, that you tarnish the Fitzroy name. You're a disappointment to your family, and to High

Society. They regard you as nothing but dirt. I've even heard that they compare you to your reckless mother."

I let out a snarl, shoving against him hard. "Do not bring my mother into this, you bastard!"

His fist slammed into my stomach, knocking the breath out of me. Pain burst through me, the blade drawing blood.

"Don't be stupid, boy," he growled.

"If you murder me, he will know," I said. "He will know. He loves me. And I love him."

"Do you?" Ben asked, gripping my hair and turning my head to the side. He let out a dark chuckle. "You love Pan? The monster that has trapped you in a marriage and has turned you into the laughing stock of the ton?"

"I love him," I whispered, my head spinning.

I *loved* him.

The thought burned through me, bringing tears to my eyes.

I did. I loved him. I was his, and he was mine. This situation was crazy, but I knew that I was meant to be with him.

The sound of a voice echoed, a shout coming through the house.

"*Pan*," I breathed. "Pan!!" I shouted.

Ben let out a low snarl, looking back at the doorway. "You bastard. Perhaps I don't need to take your life if he loves you then."

I tried to shove him back, and he put the knife away, grabbing my wrists and planting them above my head. I tried to kick at him, but his other hand grabbed my jaw.

His lips smashed against mine right as the doors to the room burst open.

"You fiend!" Pan roared.

Ben was ripped away from me and I fell to my knees, spitting on the floor and wiping my mouth with horror.

"Pan," I gasped. "Pan, it's not what it looks like."

Pan ignored me, throwing Ben across the library. He hit the shelves, books rattling and falling to the floor.

A small cadre of servants crowded in the doorway, looking on with shock.

Ben scrambled up, grinning. "We shared a *kiss*, brother. I think I might have even felt his cock harden."

"That's a lie!" I yelled.

"I challenge you to a duel," Pan growled.

"Pan," I gasped. "Pan, no."

A duel always ended in death. I stared helplessly, my heart pounding in my chest.

"Pan, please. Please no duel. Nothing happened."

Pan ignored me still, his muscles tense with rage. "Tomorrow at dawn. Highland Park. We will duel."

"If I win, I am taking him as my husband," Ben said, grinning. "And taking your crown as well."

"GET OUT!" Pan thundered.

Ben left with a smirk, pushing through those that stood in the doorway.

"Everyone leave," Pan said. "Shut the doors. Now."

They obeyed and the library doors slammed shut, leaving me alone with him.

I let out a choked sob, still on my knees. "I'm sorry—"

Pan leaned down, gripping my chin and forcing me to look at him. "Do not apologize to me."

"He was going to kill me and then he kissed me," I whispered quickly.

Tears filled my eyes, my heart feeling like it was tearing itself apart.

"Ezra," Pan said, his voice serious. "I am not angry with you."

"But we said," I gasped. "We said that we would be jealous—"

"I am not jealous. I am murderous. I am ready to behead my brother for as little as breathing on you, Ezra. You were the victim here, and I am sorry. I am deeply sorry. I still love you. Nothing has changed, except that I will have to kill him tomorrow before our wedding."

"You love me," I whispered.

Pan sighed, pulling me into his arms. He surprised me by lifting me, and I wrapped my legs around his hips and arms around his neck.

"You're a fool," he mumbled.

"I love you too," I said. "I told him that. I told him that I love you."

Pan carried me to the desk, sitting me on it. He gave me a soft look. "Do you?"

"Yes," I whispered, cupping his face. "I mean it. I have fallen for you."

Pan held my gaze, tears filling his eyes.

I leaned forward, kissing him. Wanting to wash away the memories of what had just happened, and to sink into the feeling of being with him.

Pan growled against my lips, deepening our kiss before pulling away with a moan. "Well. Now I really must murder him."

"You can't duel tomorrow," I said. "What if he wins?"

"He won't win," Pan said. "I promise he won't."

"Then mate me," I whispered. "Mate me before the duel. I want a bond with you. I want to know what it will feel like."

Pan let out a breath, closing his eyes for a moment. "Are you certain?"

"Yes," I said. "More than anything. I have never been this certain in my life."

"If I die tomorrow, then..."

"If I die with you, I will have at least tasted a slice of happiness more than I have ever before."

Pan scoffed. "We are not Shakespeare. If I die, you will be stuck with a bond and no one to fill it."

"Then don't duel."

"I must duel." Pan sighed, frustrated. "Bloody hell. This is a mess. But, I will win."

"And you will mate me," I said, raising a brow.

Pan was silent for a moment and then his shoulders relaxed, his gaze becoming heated. "You really love me, little buck?"

"Yes. Even though you drive me mad."

"Then yes, I will mate you."

He took a step back and fell to one knee, offering me his hand.

"Will you, Ezra Fitzroy III, take my mating bond?"

"Yes," I said. "Yes, I will."

Bound to the Scoundrel

P an

EZRA SPREAD OUT ON OUR BED, COMPLETELY NAKED AND waiting for me as I undressed. We had drawn the curtains, locked the doors, and I had made it known that we were not to be disturbed.

My brother would not ruin this. Tomorrow, I would have to deal with him properly, but the rest of this day belonged to me and my mate.

Ezra reached down and gripped his cock, stroking himself slowly as he watched me. I let out a low growl, my body reacting to the sight of him teasing me.

I had hoped that I would find my mate but I hadn't realized just how much he would mean to me. It had only been days since I had first seen him, and yet he had rooted himself into my very soul.

Even though I hadn't the time to prepare how I'd like, I

still had managed to gather some items to make this special. To make this what it would be if we were in my home.

"I want you," Ezra whispered.

"I want you too, little buck. Are you sure you want to try...these things?"

His eyes lit up with curiosity and he nodded. "Yes."

"If you ask me to stop, I will. At any point."

Ezra nodded again. "I trust you. But if I need us to halt, I will speak up."

"Good boy," I said, feeling a bit of pride.

It was amazing what one could find in a home that could be used for playing. Bernard, who was as well educated in carnal play as me, had managed to bring me a candle that would not burn the skin, and silk bonds for tying. He'd placed everything on a small table, along with a pitcher of fresh water should we want it.

Ezra shivered with excitement, his hand still moving over his cock. I picked up the strips of silk and went to the bed, moving him to the center.

I pulled his hand away from his cock, growling. "No more touching yourself, little buck. Give me your wrists."

"Yes, my King," he teased.

I bit my lower lip, eager to tame him. I took his wrists and leaned over, tying them together with a bond that would not harm him, and then tying him to the bedpost.

Ezra let out a breath and then whimpered, tugging on them.

"How does that feel?" I asked.

"Good," he breathed, his eyes widening. "I...I like giving the control to you."

"Good," I said. "Your trust honours me, little buck. I promise to take good care of you."

"I know," he said, watching curiously as I moved down to his ankles.

I spread his legs, binding them to opposite bed posts. I then surveyed my work, smiling to myself.

Now, he was truly helpless. He could not touch himself. He could not break away.

Fantasies ran rampant through my mind as I went back to the small table and picked up the candle. It was already burning, the wick flickering with a small flame. Red wax rolled down its sides, pooling at the bottom of the holder.

Ezra watched as I tipped it to the side, allowing the wax to drip onto my arm. It was a hot kiss, a brief burn, but it was not too hot that it would leave lasting burns. It would push him, but not harm him.

"Remind me to give Bernard my thanks," I said happily. "For he has found some items we can have fun with despite this home being empty of such things."

"I will remind you," Ezra chuckled. "You have me curious about your home in Essex. I'm not new to the knowledge of what you hint at, but I haven't experienced them firsthand."

"Remember to tell me to stop if you need me to."

"I will, Pan, but please. I want you to use me however you please. My body is yours."

"And your heart," I said, smiling as I climbed back onto the bed holding the candle.

I moved between his legs, enjoying the way he gasped as I gripped his cock for a moment, just to tease him.

"Shite," Ezra whispered.

I enjoyed his expressions change as he began to realize the predicament he was in.

He was at my mercy.

"Look at me, little buck," I said.

Our gazes locked and he relaxed almost immediately. I leaned forward, tipping the candle over his stomach.

I watched as the wax dripped, hearing him gasp as it hit his skin. My cock was already throbbing, the little noises that he made making it more so.

He strained against his bindings for a moment, letting out a helpless whimper.

"More," he rasped.

"Say please," I corrected

"More, please. *Please*."

I dripped more of the wax over his skin. I created a pattern, spreading it over his stomach and then allowing a drop to hit one of his nipples.

He immediately moaned, his hips lifting even knowing he could not go anywhere.

I smiled, enjoying taking him to the edge. I had played with wax before, but seeing his raw reactions to this new experience made me feel elated.

I gripped his cock right as I dripped more wax over his chest. He cried out, his eyes fluttering as I began to stroke him.

"You aren't allowed to cum, little buck. Not until I give you permission. Do you understand?"

"Yes," he gasped. "I will try my best."

"No. Look at me," I growled.

He looked at me, his brows drawing together.

"You *will not cum* until I allow you to."

He nodded, still writhing against his bonds. "Yes, Sir."

"Good," I purred.

I leaned down, taking the head of his cock between my lips. He let out a loud moan.

I swirled my tongue, tasting his precum. I let out a little groan of my own and then pulled back, releasing his cock.

"Please," he whispered.

"No more," I said. "Not now."

He groaned, but I dripped more wax on him. His frustration was beginning to grow, which was the goal of my endeavors.

I wanted to drive him to the edge over and over until he was begging. Truly begging. Then, and only then, would we make our bond.

My own cock would suffer in the meantime as all I wanted was to bury myself deep inside of him, but I had patience.

I would wait to breed him. I would wait to bond him.

I would wait until our souls were raw and aching.

"Pan," he cried. "I need you inside of me."

"No," I said.

I dripped more wax, drawing out gasps and whimpers from him. I leaned back, surveying the masterpiece that I had created.

I then let a drop fall on his cock.

He immediately cried out, yanking against his restraints. His cheeks flushed, his body pulling despite not being able to break free.

"Pan," he gasped.

"Do you wish for me to stop?"

He was silent for a moment, his eyes pleading. But despite his straining, there was the look of need. Of want. Of lust.

"Tell me to stop, little buck."

"No," he whispered.

"Good boy," I praised.

I dripped more wax onto his cock, chuckling at his yelps and cries. He had stopped caring if anyone could hear us, forgetting about the world around us.

108

Another red drop of wax covered his cock and he gasped.

"I'm so close to cumming."

"Are you?" I asked.

"Yes."

I pulled the candle back and slid off the bed, hiding my grin at his horrified gasp.

"But I'm so close!"

"Yes, I know," I chuckled, setting the candle back down on the table. "We must ensure you only cum when I allow you. I can't risk pushing you too far. Yet."

"Monster," he groaned. "You fiend. You devil."

"I am all of those things," I teased.

I went to the sink in our room, grabbing a towel and dampening it with water. I went back to my fiancé, climbing onto the bed between his legs.

He glared at me now, which gave me a little thrill. I did like it when he was angry at me during our lovemaking, it made it so much sweeter when he finally submitted.

"You look as if you hate me, little buck," I said with a grin.

"Go to hell," he mumbled.

I ran the warm towel over his body, wiping away the wax. I took my time to take it off his skin, rubbing his nipples in careful circles.

His head fell back on the cushions, his breath hitching.

He muttered a curse as I continued, working until all that was left was his cock.

I ran the towel over it, gripping him. He gasped, his head lifting as I carefully removed the wax.

"This is torture," he groaned.

"The best kind," I said.

I cleaned off the last of the wax and then leaned down, giving the head of his cock a single lick.

"Oh you *ARE* evil!" he growled in disbelief.

"Evil is fun, little buck. Especially when that evil is based in carnal desires."

He yanked against his restraints as I tossed the towel to the side.

"Pan!"

I was waiting to see how long it would take before he realized that honey caught more flies than vinegar.

"You bastard," he growled.

I ran my fingertips down his cock and then over his balls, down to his hole. His movements stilled, his pants turning into another small moan.

"So helpless," I said, teasing him with my fingers.

I circled his hole whilst holding his gaze.

His cheeks turned even more red, his eyes wide.

"I thought you wanted this, little buck," I whispered. "To give in to me. Why are you fighting so hard?"

He glared as I continued to tease him. Silence settled between us for moments, but then he frowned.

"Oh," he whispered.

The realization that overtook him made my cock pulse.

"I want you," he breathed. "I want you to control when I cum."

"There we go," I purred.

I pushed one finger inside of him, giving him a taste of the reward he'd get for being good.

His expression melted, his moan softening.

"I'm yours. I'm thankful for your touch and for everything that you do to me."

"Even when I drip hot wax on your pulsing cock?"

"Yes," he rasped. "Even then."

"Good boy," I said, giving him another finger.

I moved them in and out of him, teasing him gently. Readying him for my cock.

"Do you like it when I tease you?"

"*Yes.*"

"Ask for more then. Politely."

Ezra groaned, but he obeyed. "Please give me more. Whatever you think I deserve. *Please.*"

"That was not a question, little buck."

He let out a frustrated noise, but cut it off before I could raise a brow. "Will you please give me what you think I need?"

Now, I grinned.

I reached over and untied one ankle, and then the other, allowing his legs to be free. I then leaned over the bed, reaching for the small pitcher of oil on the nightstand. I poured some into my hands, and then rubbed it over my cock and settled back between his legs.

I teased him again, using the oil to make sure he was ready.

"Do you want to remain tied?" I asked.

"I want to touch you," he breathed.

I nodded and undid the ties around his wrists, allowing him to be free.

His legs wrapped around my hips, his arms around my neck. He pulled me into a kiss, a desperate one.

I couldn't wait any longer.

"I need you," I breathed.

"I need you too," he said, kissing me again.

I reached between us, guiding my cock against him. He moaned as I pushed inside of him, filling him with my cock.

"All of you," he gasped.

I growled, thrusting my hips forward to fill him completely.

"I love you," I said. "I love you so much, Ezra."

"I love you too," he groaned.

I began to move, finding a slow rhythm that allowed me to give him every inch with each stroke. He held on to me, our lips finding each other in a deep kiss. Our tongues met, our bodies melding together.

I felt the need to bond, to mate. I felt that primal urge rise up again, but this time I gave into it fully.

He groaned as my body began to shift into my beast form, and he surprised me by reaching up to grip my horns. I began to fuck him harder, to drive in and out of him with a reckless need.

"Mate me," he gasped. "Please mate me."

"Yes," I rasped.

I kissed him again, and then kissed down to his neck. "This might hurt," I whispered. "Mating bonds are bites..."

"Do it," he said, his grip on me tightening.

I took a deep breath, slowing my rhythm. I was so close to cumming, so close to filling him.

I sank my teeth into his shoulder. He gasped in my ear and then moaned, his arms still bound around me.

I felt his teeth sink into my chest, returning the bite. There was a brief sting, but then I felt a flood of pleasure unlike anything I had ever known.

I drew back with a gasp as our bond came to life, the string of fate that tied our souls together burning like lightning.

I could feel *him*. His emotions, his needs, his wants. I could feel the passion between us, how *good* being together felt.

I began to drive into him again, the two of us moaning together.

"Cum with me," I gasped, reaching between us.

Pleasure burned through us as I touched him, stroking his cock as I drove into him.

"Cum for me."

"Yes, Sir," he cried.

His words sent me over the edge. He cried out as I did, the two of us cumming together.

I filled him, giving him every last drop until I was finished. I held up my hand, licking his own cum from my fingers.

I let out a pant, relaxing.

"I can feel you," he whispered in wonder.

I smiled, feeling him through our bond. I held my hand to his heart, feeling the beat.

"Can you feel how much I love you?"

"Yes," he said.

Tears filled his eyes and he held his hand over mine, holding it to him.

"Now you can never rid yourself of me," he teased. "Forever bound to the scoundrel."

Wed to the Satyr King

E^{zra}

Fog clung to the gardens, the grass dewy as the sun began to peek over Westminster. Nerves worked through me as I stood next to Bernard, the two of us waiting with Pan.

"This is illegal," I said.

I was trying to control my fears, to trust that Pan would be okay.

Pan was pacing back and forth, obviously already angry. I could feel it too, which was the most bizarre thing in this world to me.

Our mated bond tied us together, pairing our souls. Our emotions echoed each other, and I knew that he was doing his best to remain calm and collected.

"Don't worry, Prince Ezra," Bernard said. "Our King will succeed. We have a wedding today, this will be a memory come noon."

Bernard was so sure, but I was not. Pan's brother was a bastard, and he would not duel fairly.

We heard rustling and looked up to see the devil coming our way through the trees. There was another fellow with him holding a box that must have carried the gun he planned to use.

Pan glared at him, his arms crossed behind his back. "Ben. We don't have to do this, and I would like to offer you the chance to bow out."

"And miss out on..." His brother drifted off, his nostrils flaring. "You *mated* him?! The human?!"

"Yes," Pan said. "The crown is secure."

I had forgotten about that. I didn't let my expression waver though. I was thankful to be mated, and thankful to have Pan by my side.

I wanted this to be over already.

"Let us duel then," Ben snarled.

"We must have our weapons inspected. Bernard will inspect yours, and your...person will inspect mine."

Ben nodded, glaring at Pan.

Bernard and the other fellow did just that, exchanging boxes so that they could inspect the guns.

"Everything is proper," Bernard said.

The other man nodded in agreement.

"Very well," Pan said.

I felt a flutter of nerves as Pan and Ben went to retrieve their weapons. They then stood back to back, their expressions steeled.

I felt fear again. Fear that I would lose the life I had just found, the love I had just discovered.

Pan glanced over at me—and the bastard *winked*.

What on earth did he have planned?!

"Begin!" Bernard said.

I held my breath as Pan and Ben began to walk their paces.

Suddenly, I heard shouts echoing through the gardens, but that did not stop Pan or Ben.

It also did not stop Ben from turning three paces early.

"NO!" I shouted, but it was too late.

Ben took his shot, the sound of the gun firing cracking through the air.

The bullet sailed straight past Pan.

Pan turned with a grin, tossing his gun to Bernard, who caught it and stowed it away in the bushes just in time for Pan to hold up his hands.

A group of Queen's guards burst through the trees, immediately tackling Ben to the ground.

"These men have attacked us!" Pan exclaimed. "He has shot at a King!"

Ben's fellow took off running, only for two more guards to come through and take off after him.

I stared in shock as chaos broke out.

Pan came over to me, pulling me close. "Ben has never been a good shot."

"You set me up!" Ben roared, trying to kick the guards free.

"Good bye, brother!" Pan exclaimed. "Have fun with the Queen's guard."

I watched in shock as he was taken away, the guards working together to drag him off.

"You should have told me!" I exclaimed.

Pan turned me, pulling me close. I swat at his arm, but pulled my hand away with blood.

"It struck you!!"

"It merely grazed me," Pan snorted.

"You are bleeding!!!"

"I am fine, my love," Pan snickered. "So concerned!"

"Bernard!" I said helplessly.

"We will get him patched up," Bernard chuckled.

"Now," Pan said, smirking. "Now that he is taken care of, I have a scoundrel to wed."

~

IT WASN'T TWO HOURS LATER THAT I FOUND MYSELF STANDING in front of my family and the Archbishop with Pan. My cousin Phoebe and her new monster husband, Ambrose, stood off to the side.

I hoped that Ambrose would be as good to her as Pan was to me.

My monstrous mate.

My soon to be husband.

The duel had ended in his brother being arrested and taken off, along with being banned from the Land of Essex again, and ultimately no longer being a problem.

I was dressed in a nice waistcoat, one that was purple and embroidered with golden thread. Pan was wearing a similar outfit, the two of us making a picturesque couple.

My father had finally seemed to have accepted that I was getting married, and hadn't made any untoward comments.

I was finally breaking away from the name of the Fitzroys.

I could feel Pan's happiness through our bond, love and excitement overflowing for the life that lay ahead of us. This sennight had been a whirlwind, one that had swept me onto a path only fate could have paved.

Pan took my hand, holding a golden band to my finger. The whole world melted away, and I found myself falling into everything that was him.

"With this ring I thee wed, with my body I thee worship, and with all my worldly goods I thee endow. I promise to protect you, to love you, and to cherish you until the end of time."

His words brought tears to my eyes. He slid the ring on my finger, offering me a soft smile.

I took the other ring, holding it to his finger, and said my vows.

"With this ring I thee wed, with my body I thee worship, and with all my worldly goods I thee endow. I promise to love you, to be there for you in times of trouble, and to cherish you even when you drive me mad."

Pan chuckled as I slid the ring on.

The Archbishop began his speech about marriage, but I didn't listen to any of it. His voice drolled on and on, but I was lost in the gaze of my monstrous mate.

Finally, he was finished.

Pan grinned, drawing me close. Our lips met, our first kiss shared in marriage.

I was officially wed to the Satyr King.

Two Months Later

E zra

*The Satyr King and his Prince, the darlings of Essex,
will be hosting their very own Summer Ball. This author
has waited most patiently to see how the Monster King and
his Fated Mate have continued their lives after such scandalous beginnings, and will be eager to report the festivities
of the evening.*
— *Lady Grey, The High Tea*

"HUSBAND, MY LOVE, HAVE YOU SEEN OUR ROPES FOR
bondage? And where in the seven hells have the paddles
gone? I want to secure them before our guests arrive."

I smirked as I waited for Pan to find me. I was in the

room we had deemed our Room of Passion, and I was already naked and waiting for him on the lush bed.

He'd been so busy this sennight, taking care of his kingly duties, while I had found myself becoming more and more comfortable in my role as a prince. For the first time in my life, I found myself helping others, and not hating it.

It was hard to believe that it had only been two months since the whirlwind of our engagement and marriage, but I had found more happiness than I thought possible.

"Ezra!"

Pan came around the corner, freezing in the doorway as his eyes laid upon me.

"Seven hells," he breathed.

He was already dressed for the party, which made my plan all the more devious.

I grinned as his cock immediately hardened in his breeches. He made a noise and then stepped into the room, shutting the double doors behind him.

"My love. We are preparing for our very own party," he said. "The guests will arrive soon!"

"I can get dressed if you'd like," I teased. "I just wanted to please you before our festivities began."

Pan rolled his eyes dramatically, but his lips were already twisted into a smile.

"You're such a needy little Prince, aren't you? Can't even wait until after our party tonight."

"Very needy," I said. "I've been thinking about taking you all morning, but you were so busy.

My cock throbbed in response, standing straight up.

Pan cursed again, flustered. "My apologies, little buck, for being so busy," he murmured. He raised a brow, his heated gaze taking me in. "You're breathtaking."

Our dynamic over the last two months had settled into

an exciting adventure. Most days, Pan liked to lead, but I also enjoyed surprising him. It threw him off guard, and there was nothing more appealing than my flustered monster.

"Are you going to devour me, my King?" I asked.

"You devil," he chuckled. "Come here. Kneel in front of me."

I slid off the bed and went to him, kneeling at his hooves.

"Undress me and take my cock."

"Yes, Sir," I said, smirking.

I reached up, undoing the buttons of his breeches. Pan let out a groan as I ran my hand over his cock through the fabric before pulling them down, letting it free.

I leaned forward, taking the head of his cock between my lips. I sucked him, swirling my tongue just the way he loved.

"Little buck," he said huskily. "My love, I have no control today and we don't have much time."

"I want you to cum so that I may taste you on my lips while I talk to the members of the ton."

Pan cursed, letting out a groan. "You are perfect, little buck."

I gripped the base of his cock and then began to suck him, taking him as far down my throat as possible. His fingers curled into my hair, holding my head as he moaned.

He began to thrust, the feral noises he made making me hard.

Tears filled my eyes as I swallowed him, his hands holding me in place.

I loved it when he took control like this. When he used my mouth and body.

"I need to be inside you," he gasped.

He pulled free of my mouth and I dragged in a harsh breath as he scooped me up. He took me to the bed, bending me over the side.

"I'm already ready for you," I breathed.

"You knew I couldn't resist," Pan grunted, pressing the head of his cock against me.

It was true, I had known that.

I smirked in victory as he thrust inside of me, pleasure bursting through my body. I cried out as his cock filled me completely, driving inside of me.

He pushed my torso down onto the bed, gripping my hips hard as he began to fuck me.

"Such a perfect ass," he huffed, letting out a soft moan. "My perfect mate."

"Breed me," I grunted, fighting the urge to beg him over and over. "Now your cum will be inside of me during the party. Remember, we're the darlings of Essex."

Pan growled, pumping into me harder. "Such *scandalous* beginnings."

The High Tea came in handy for once, sending my mate into an even more passionate frenzy. I groaned as he continued to thrust, the bed creaking from our raw lovemaking.

"I'm going to fill you," he growled.

"Please!" I cried.

He reached around to stroke my cock, making me cry out.

"Cum for me, my love," he gasped.

My King's wish was my command. My voice echoed through the room as my climax overtook me, my cum shooting out as Pan started to cum as well.

He filled me, his hot seed saturating me in its warmth. I

groaned, my head spinning with euphoria as I collapsed onto the bed.

Pan leaned against me, letting out a deep chuckle. "You drive me wild, little buck. Open your mouth."

I obeyed him, turning my head so that I could suck my cum from his fingers. His cock was still buried deep inside of me.

I gasped as he gave a small thrust.

"You're still hard."

"I am," Pan said. "I think...I think we might be late to our very own party, little buck."

"I think society would expect nothing less from the Scoundrel and the Satyr King."

Clio's Creatures

Hello Creatures!

My name is Clio Evans and I am so excited to introduce myself to you! I'm a lover of all things that go bump in the night, fancy peens, coffee, and chocolate.

IF you had the chance to be matched with a monster-what kind would you choose?!

Let me know by joining me on FB and Instagram. I'm a sucker for werewolves (and plague doctors ;)) to this day.

Also by Clio Evans

CREATURE CAFE SERIES

Little Slice of Hell

Little Sip of Sin

Little Lick of Lust

Little Shock of Hate

Little Piece of Sass

Little Song of Pain

Little Taste of Need

Little Risk of Fall

Little Wings of Fate

Little Souls of Fire

Little Kiss of Snow: A Creature Cafe Christmas Anthology

WARTS & CLAWS INC. SERIES

Not So Kind Regards

Not So Best Wishes

Not So Thanks in Advance

Not So Yours Truly

Not So Much Appreciated

FREAKS OF NATURE DUET

Doves & Demons

Demons & Doves (coming Fall 2023)

THREE FATES MAFIA SERIES

Thieves & Monsters

Killers & Monsters

Villains & Monsters

Queens & Monsters

Heroes & Monsters

Printed in Great Britain
by Amazon